A Crock of Sundries

Volume One

prose, poetry, and plays by
Timothy R. Baldwin

INDIES UNITED PUBLISHING HOUSE, LLC

Published by Indies United Publishing House, LLC

ISBN-13: 978-1-64456-345-8 (paperback)
ISBN-13: 978-1-64456-346-5 (mobi)
ISBN 13: 978-1-64456-347-2 (ePub)

Library of Congress Control Number: 2021941537

INDIES UNITED PUBLISHING HOUSE, LLC
P.O. BOX 3071
QUINCY, IL 62305-3071
www.indiesunited.net

To the aspiring writer:
You will never truly master the craft of writing, but your work tomorrow will always be better than it was today.
Write on!

I
A Lasting Heirloom

In Meme and Story

Creative Nonfiction:

An Essay on Writing

Look up writing quotes by Flannery O'Conner, and you'll find a plethora of ways in which she describes the writing process. Statements include everything from writing being a terrible experience to writing being some means by which the author discovers deep-seated truths.

Indeed, one could expeditiously launch a similar search on such writers as Ernest Hemmingway, Annie Dillard, or Langston Hughes. Perhaps upon a philosophical bent, one could even go so far as to decontextualize the quote, create a meme, and post said meme on their social media account, proclaiming, "A-ha! This is my truth as well!"

Yet, the perpetrator of the said meme will be guilty of pretext, lazily using someone else's words on the pretense of intellectual ingenuity instead of doing the hard work of creating their meaning.

As Shakespeare once said, "Brevity is the soul of whit!" So let my long words express my shorter meaning.

In writing, I have plumbed the depths of my beliefs in a cathartic attempt to exorcise mendacious wordplay and get to the very heart of truth. Most of these verbal meanderings have gone unpublished, left to simmer in solitude in anticipation of some promised excavation of the mind. Such long-forgotten literary musings lay in wake until, like Dr. Frankenstein, I haphazardly attempt to incorporate new ideas with the old while lacking the courage or the patience to start the work from the very beginning, as many great artists are wont to experience.

From Van Gogh to Fitzgerald, such great artists never in their lifetime experienced the fame and fortune amassed as a result of their great masterpieces. Van Gogh only sold one painting in his lifetime, and Fitzgerald's The Great Gatsby didn't take off until long after he was dead. Yet both masters poured themselves, heart and soul, into every jot and tittle of their masterpieces. Dare I compare myself to these masters as I painstakingly piece sentence after sentence in what I hope to be my most remarkable work yet?

To date, I have published four full-length works and a handful of short stories and poems in anthologies or quarterly magazines. All of these works represent a truth about myself and the way I see the world around me. They are a result of the courage, patience, and hope I've poured onto the pages through systematic planning and revision. Before I set out to take up the helm of another literary project, I dawdle as the idea develops. Somewhere in the back of my mind, the idea is waiting for its awakening as I engross myself in the sum-total of someone else's painstaking process.

Now to why I write. Is it necessary for me to write? Probably not. Did Van Gogh have to cut off his ear? Did Fitzgerald have to carve a piece of himself into the pages of his masterpiece? Probably not. Yet, they both did what they did for love, as do I. I also pray that you, my dear reader, enjoy the end product as much as I enjoyed the process that got us to the point of literary convergence.

I started as most great artists do, learning from the greats. Growing up, my mother instilled within me a love for reading. She'd devour and share with me one book after another, taking equal pleasure in simply crafted stories and the far more meritorious works of C.S. Lewis or J. R. R. Tolkien.

However, my real reading journey evolved into writing when a colleague of mine published his first novel. After all, if he could do it, then why couldn't I do the same? My writing is and always has been representative of the encouragement of my friends, family, and teachers. They are people who make up a tapestry of dedicated support, from elementary school through college and post-graduate work.

It's been a loving journey, a culmination of everything I have read, seen, and experienced in life. I borrowed a little bit of style from one author over here and incorporated a little bit of craft from an author over there, all of it mixed with a bit of flair of my own.

Indeed, during my life, I never once, and at no specific moment in time, did I ever realize that I enjoyed writing per se. I just did, do, and always will. It's a flow, a process, and a point to which I strive for perfection with no end in sight. Each piece may be distinct to my reader, but for me, each is a chapter in my story—each piece representing what I've learned along the way and poured into each subsequent literary work.

Starting another story can be a thing of great procrastination. Yet, I love being in the thick of the process - one that is as soothing as it is savage. As much as an author becomes attached to the ingenuity of his own words, an author must rip out those words when they fail to serve the narrative. Thus creating a sort of dichotomy for the author, existing as both master and slave to the story.

The story. These stories. At some point, they will exist apart from me, becoming a permanent record of who I was and how I saw the world at the time of writing. Perhaps that is why I write. Or maybe I'm hoping some reader will find great profundity in my words and see fit to quote me in a decontextualized meme with a nonsensical background like pink balloons or a vector illustration of a man skiing. Or, even better, photoshop one of many publicly available photos of myself while attributing to me some unsound advice about writing that I would only say long after I'm dead. Regardless, even without observation, I will always write on.

I, Lamppost

A Poem

I feel like a lamppost.
Mounted on a shady street corner,
I stand tall and upright,
a radiant light,
in a pitch-black night.

Some take notice of me.
As the night engulfs the day,
my light is sought and found,
by those with the eyes to see
and appreciate my illumination.
Though sometimes it's blinding,
causing discomfort,

leaving those wanderers blinking,
until with adjusted eyes peering,
they see with my radiance
through the darkness.

Other times my light is pale,
a soft comfort
to those wandering night souls
in search of some sense
in an otherwise dark world.

I am a lamppost,
spotted with rust and chipped paint,
covered by yellowed, tattered flyers -
pictures of lost pets,
posters of garage sales,
and alluring announcements.
Though weathered by years
and holding onto memories,
my light does not wane,
but casts out night's fears.

I have seen so much,
I have been used
by so many.
Yet I am here,
giving light to any
who would draw near,
seeking solace and comfort
in the light

which shines
amidst the dark hours
of life's expedition.

My Not Favorite Teacher

A Poem

I looked up at him
With my best stern
look, sassy
look, a look
that told him I was serious.
Standing jaunty like
with arms
on hips, feet
wide apart, head
slightly cocked,
and wide eyes.

Tight lips
with a downward curve.
Just like my momma shows me
every time I get in trouble.

Which is often. I mean:
only sometimes, and
maybe never.
I'm a good girl. Really!
Even when my teacher calls
home and speaks to momma
through an interpreter.

I didn't do nothing. That's why
I stand there staring
scowling, and showing
my teacher. I mean:
I'm serious. He's my favorite,
but now he's not.
I'm in trouble with momma,
so he's in trouble with me.

So I stand and stare
like momma scowls
at me, just waiting
for him to say… something.
But you know what
he said:
"What's that look for?"
And my reply:

a frown and an upward
tilt of my head
and a jut of my jaw.
But he says nothing,
so you know what I said?
I said:
"You should know."

And he
he just
just smiled
and said
Nothing.

Can you believe the nerve? But I just
walked, no
stomped in silence
away from him
my not favorite teacher.

Pondering

Creative Nonfiction

Growing up, I had a small collection of buttons. I would proudly wear my buttons for a day. I even pinned a few to my bookbag just to be one of the cool kids. At school, there was always that one kid who plastered her bag with a monumental medley of colors and images, causing others to wonder whether a bag even existed beneath the collage of pins strapped to her back.

Nonetheless, buttons were a great way to dress up the faded bag handed down to you by your older brother or sister. Smiley faces and peace signs would be used to hide the bag's blemishes and draw attention away from the fraying nylon. Then, to personalize your bag, you would include buttons of your favorite bands. Maybe KISS, Green Day, or even the New Kids on the Block were included in your envied menagerie pinned to the back of your bag. Whatever you had, your buttons represented the places you visited and the things you loved. Each button was a timeless memento printed on a thin paper disc, shrink-wrapped on a cheap piece of tin, and lovingly pinned to your bag.

I once thought these cheap but fun little trinkets had passed their prime in favor of their modern counterparts, the meme. But a meme you cannot hold. A meme existing only in digital format does not possess the palpable immortality inherent within a button.

In one of my teaching assignments, I had the privilege of observing the teaching of critical thinking in action. I chose a Foundations of Technology (FOT) Class to observe and jot down my observations. Armed with a notepad, I was ready to take notes to help create a continuum of conversation around the topic of increasing levels of critical thinking in our school-wide instruction. FOT fit two requirements: outside of my content area and taking place during my planning period.

During this class, tenth-grade students were to create buttons using a template on Microsoft Word. Already populated with a sample image, the students had to find images on the web or clipart and replace the sample image with an image they found on the internet. Once found, students carelessly copied this image without giving credit to the source. Not much critical thinking took place during this class unless I count the times students screwed up the template and had to figure out how to fix it, or simply gave up (or didn't try) and opted instead to ask the instructor or a friend for help.

Nonetheless, I walked around the room, going through the motions of putting tally marks on various and vague descriptions of behaviors I observed being demonstrated by the teacher and the students. Did the students identify a problem and try to solve it using more than one method?

Did the students persevere until they solved the problem? Did the teacher ask open-ended questions? Did the teacher give students a real-world problem to which they had to apply real-world skills? To be honest, I thought it was a stretch, but I did my best to find the critical thinking, however minute, in everything the students were doing.

For about ten minutes, I continued my rounds of observation and note-taking, managing to apply a great deal more critical thinking than the total of students in the room. Most simply chose pictures they copied and pasted into the template, quickly manipulating it into an accent ring. Not much thinking, critical or otherwise, seemed to be occurring. Maybe that was the point. Perhaps it was I who was supposed to think critically in my mission to discover critical thinking.

In my mission to discover active critical thinking, I came across a student named Ryan from my English class. Ryan managed to find several pictures of myself on the Internet, which is not that hard to do with a quick name search. If you'd like, you can do an internet search for my name, and you will find numerous pictures of me. These you can also download, but I'm not sure why you would want to. But this kid did. He copied the image, pasted it into the template, and then looked up to see that I was looking at his work.

"Sure," I said. "If you really want to use my face, you can. No need to ask my permission."

He got the hint, then asked for permission. I obliged his request because I didn't care one way or the other. When I left after doing my rounds of critical thinking observation, I headed to my office, then reflected upon my findings. When I finished, I dropped the peer observation on a pile somewhere in my office, knowing that it would become one more thing we had to do, though no one would follow up and hold us accountable for the work. Like the paper, I completely forgot about my picture potentially being used for some kid's button project.

I forgot, that is, until several weeks later. I began class in the usual way with a witty remark, followed by an object, followed by the lesson. As I spoke, a familiar glint off Ryan's t-shirt caught my attention. I paused, noting his buddy Andrew sported a similar glint. Playful grins formed on their faces as they waited, eyes locked with my own, for a reaction.

"I see you found a second picture," I said to Ryan.

"Yes," he said, "And I made one for Andrew. I figured he'd want one once he saw mine."

Looking at the two buttons pinned to their t-shirts, I noticed Ryan's button had a caption below my face:

"PONDER"

And so I did. And in my pondering, I concluded that I have certainly made quite a lasting impression on these two students. I imagine they will have those buttons for years to come, and they will one day, maybe in twenty years, be cleaning out a junk drawer, and each will find his button, respectively. They will ponder and, in their pondering, they will tell their kids about this teacher who allowed himself to be buttoned. Thus, my image will become a lasting heirloom, passed on from one generation to the next.

II
One Generation to the Next

Generations

A Poem

Around the table
It's what we do when
my family gets together.
My father says, just like his before,
"Wanna play a game?"

When my grandfather was alive
it was a card game. Any really.
Canasta, Spades, Pitch, or Poker.
Always his rules.
Even when his were wrong.
So I discovered
when my brother looked up the rules.

But today.
Today I play with my father.
His game:
Backgammon.

I learned to play when I was young.
My father teaching my brother and me.
We didn't know if
he, like his father,
made them up, or if
he played by the rules.
My brother and I
We looked them up once
to confirm
our preteen suspicions.
We were just old enough
to recognize when our grandfather
was full of shit and therefore
conclude our father might be too.
He wasn't.

But it doesn't matter now.
Not as I take my place
across from my father.
A place where he sat as his father
aged on into glory.
Two generations of men
father and son
making up lost years

over a simple game.

In twenty years
I will be where my father
once sat before his own.
But today.
Today I play with my father.
He is happy.
And so am I.

One Hundred Words

Creative Nonfiction: Memoir

We spoke no more than 100 words to each other over the course of twenty years, and the time we spent together amounted to no more than a few days. It should come as no surprise that I have very few vivid memories of my grandfather, and the ones I have are like the edges of an old photograph, frayed and stained by age - an uneven yellow, almost brown tinge like someone dipped it in cold black coffee and left it out to dry in the sun.

When he died, my grandfather left his

material legacy behind - a two-story house and a two-car garage, both with matching blue paint fading and peeling, along with one of those fifteen-foot contractor vans with the two windows in the rear. This van, brown with gaping rusty holes, rattled as he drove it from neighborhood to neighborhood picking up from the side of the road broken washing machines, old computers, scrap metal, and anything he thought might be of use or value to him one day. These he would stash, stack, or stuff in his garage or house. His garage seemed to spew forth his treasures while towers of boxes within his house threatened to topple over. I know this because I rode in the front seat of the van while he made one stop before dropping me off at home.

It was a hot August day. My mother told my brother and me that she had arranged for my grandfather, her father, to pick us from soccer practice that afternoon. When the time came, all of our teammates and our coaches left us alone. In the green desert of our high school's sports complex, my brother and I baked, sweaty and thirsty. We waited, deciding this man we both barely knew had forgotten about us. At this point, we walked until we reached the crest of the hill leading out to the surrounding neighborhood, where we saw the van.

I recognized the van and its driver before my brother did. Or, more accurately, I chose to acknowledge my grandfather, whereas my brother bluntly refused to get in the vehicle. He walked home, and I rode with my grandfather. The van shook and rattled while an old microwave, caked with dust and grease, crashed across the floor as we bounced over potholes until my grandfather spotted a pile of garbage sparkling in the afternoon sun. Without asking if I minded, he stopped the van, cranked the emergency brake, and got out without closing his door. The rear door creaked open, and one, two, three pieces of scrap metal slid in, along with another microwave and a filthy computer. The rear door creaked shut with a slam, and my grandfather was back in the van. He looked at me, chuckled gruffly, and said, "That's a good find."

Years later, long after my grandfather died, my parents were dumping their surplus of coffee mugs. I took the two that belonged to my grandfather, a matching set with a cartoon picture of two gloved hands holding a porter cable grinder applying pressure to a pile of coffee beans. The image is captioned in bold lettering: FRESH GROUND COFFEE. When company comes, I serve them coffee in these mugs. They chuckle. And I tell them, these belonged to my grandfather. Indeed, he was a man who truly saw treasure in what others would dismiss as junk.

Though I never really knew the man, I am fascinated, nonetheless. He was a man who, I believe, had a reason for everything he did. He loved the wild, or so I heard. Though I don't remember the details, I am told he went camping with us. Attached to this experience is a memory, cloudy and faded with time, of learning how to fish. We had set up beneath a shade of trees upon a lake. He showed my brother and me how to wrap a worm and apply pressure to the squirming muscle until the spear-like end pierced through with a pop. Then we cast off our rods, and he let us alone. When we needed help, he came to us, gently showing us again how to set and cast our line and wait a silent eternity until we felt a tug. And there, beneath the shade, he would help us gently reel in our line, inspect our catch, then toss it back in. It was not about catching fish, so much as it was about being there as one generation passed on a legacy to another. Perhaps he passed on to us one lesson in what I imagine to be potentially countless others in learning how to survive for days, if not weeks, with just a pocketknife, a fishing rod, and a frugal use of words.

A Froggy Will

Creative Nonfiction: Memoir

My earliest memories of catching frogs are set in the foreground of my grandparent's camp, their marshy lawn sloshing on my shoes and soaking my socks.

One afternoon my grandmother took me outside to play a game of scoop ball. One plays this game using scoop bats, which resemble a lacrosse stick, only small enough to be held and operated with one hand. As my grandmother and I tossed the ball with our scoop bats, my brother remained inside.

There, I imagine he sat in the dim light of the kitchen, refusing to eat the soup my grandparents made for lunch that day. Clearly not my parent's cooking, the homemade soup consisted of a watery broth, various vegetables, and tiny shreds of chicken. I had initially complained about the food.

"It's too watery," I had said as I stirred pieces of mushy carrots and soggy celery around the tasteless broth. "I thought it would be thicker, like a stew."

"Well, it's not," my grandfather barked. "Eat it."

My brother curled his lips and glared. "No."

"Well, I guess you two will just sit there until you eat it," my grandmother said.

Presented with no other option, I managed to down the food without further complaint. My brother was not as cooperative. On top of being a picky eater, he possessed an iron-clad will that needed to be coaxed rather than forced open. My grandfather, never the coaxing type, remained inside waging a war of wills with my brother.

Meanwhile, my grandmother and I

went outside. She'd toss a whiffle ball toward me. I'd extend my scoop bat and once again fail to catch the ball. Though my grandmother would tell me to get in front of the ball countless times, my feet would remain firmly planted in the marshy ground. Then I'd overthrow the ball, paying for my carelessness by running after it and trying it again.

Eventually, the screen door opened with a creak to reveal my brother, lips drawn tight as he promenaded down the steps. Behind him, the door swung shut. A giant hand caught the door and my grandfather, pushing the door open, tramped down the steps after my brother.

"Hey, Peter," my grandfather barked. "You didn't finish."

"Let him alone for now," my grandmother said as my brother put distance between himself and my grandfather.

"Eh? Well, he won't get anything later."

"Why don't you wait inside on the porch."

Tromping back inside, my grandfather plopped himself on a dingy-white wicker chair as he waited for my grandmother. Meanwhile, my grandmother showed my brother how to use the scoop ball. For a moment, she watched us toss and miss the ball several times before one landed with a satisfying thwack into my scoop. Satisfied, my grandmother joined my grandfather on the porch. As my brother and I silently tossed and overthrew the ball, we could hear the muffled whispers of my grandmother and my grandfather's voice, which seemed unable to achieve a volume lower than a suppressed roar.

Deciding we had enough of the game, my brother and I set the ball and scoop bats down in favor of exploring the yard. A clothesline seemed to curtain the yard in, especially with a white sheet draped over the line and flapping in the breeze. Beyond the white curtain, there was a brown boat shed. From there, a dock led toward the lake. As we walked toward the boat shed, my brother and I discovered the drainage ditch, a barrier between my grandparents' yard and their neighbor's yard. Walking toward the drainage ditch, droplets of water splashed up from the ground, dampening my socks and legs. As I took another step, hundreds of frogs leaped in the air and away from my deadly feet. Stopping, I placed my hands on my knees to examine my find. I called my brother over.

"Peter, come here."

Trotting and splashing, my brother created living waves in the marshy drainage ditch as frog after frog leaped toward me.

"I want to catch one," my brother said as both of his hands snatched at the water in front of him, causing a frog to leap a safe distance away from him. Splashing another heavy foot down in front of him, he executed the same motion, which resulted in the same outcome, hands filled with grass and mud, but no frog. My gentle splashings and slow careless snatchings yielded similar results — a lot of green amphibious bodies hopping away as I successfully caught clumps of mud-covered grass.

"You'll never catch anything like that," my grandmother called.

My brother and I stopped our tromping and stood erect. As we wiped mud, grass, and water on our shorts, we waited for our grandmother's scolding. Instead, she came toward us carrying cups made of thin, rigid plastic.

"If you're going to catch frogs, you have to stay still in one place," she said. Then, demonstrating from the dry ground, she continued to explain. "Hold the cup from the bottom with one hand. Cup the other hand and make it ready to close in on top of the cup." As she explained and demonstrated this procedure, my grandfather came out with a grimy painter's bucket, which he dipped in the drainage ditch, partially filling it with murky water.

"Here. Put the frogs in here when you've caught them," my grandfather said.

Armed with plastic cups and their approval, my brother and I attempted once again to catch frogs.

I crept behind my first victim. Its head and eyes poked above the water while its body remained submerged in the swamp. I held the bottom of the cup in my left hand and brought the open end of the cup behind the dark slick body of the frog. Parallel to the cup, I stiffened my palm and fingers, anticipating my first catch of the day. Inching closer to the frog, I closed in on the frog.

"Now. Trap the frog as quick as you can," my grandmother whispered.

In one quick awkward movement, I slammed cup and hand together, only to come up empty.

"Try again," my grandmother coached. "But come from the sides."

Stepping closer to the frog with my best attempt at stealth, I brought the cup and my hand closer to the frog, flanking it on either side. With steady speed, I closed my right hand over the top of the cup.

"You catch anything?" my grandfather barked.

Moving a finger to the side, just wide enough to peek through my hand and into the cup, I saw the slimy body of a frog, throat pulsating in rapid movements as its dark left eye stared back at me.

"Yeah," I said as I marched over to the bucket, holding my cup high so my brother and grandparents could see. With the top of the cup covered by my right hand, I lowered the cup into the bucket and released my catch.

That afternoon, my grandparents

stood on the lawn watching my brother and me make one muddy attempt after another to catch enough frogs to fill the bucket my grandfather brought out for us. By the time we had to clean up for dinner, the bottom of the bucket seemed to hop with the life of slimy amphibious bodies piled on top of each other.

"Timmy," my grandmother said, peering into the bucket. "How many did you and Peter catch?"

"Twenty-six? I can't tell," I said. "They're moving too much."

"Good job," my grandmother said.

"I'm hungry," my brother said.

"Good," my grandfather barked. "It's time to get cleaned up for dinner."

"What're we having?" my brother said.

My grandfather locked eyes with my brother. "Chicken, green beans, and mashed potatoes. You gonna eat those?"

My brother nodded.

"Good," my grandfather said.

My grandfather grabbed the bucket and dumped a hopping waterfall of slime and mud into the swampy drainage ditch. My grandmother led my brother and me into the cabin, where we took a bath and changed into soft, floral-scented pajamas. Sitting down to eat, my grandfather prayed for the meal. As we ate, my brother stabbed, prodded, and poked at his food, eventually eating every piece of baked chicken, green beans, and mashed potatoes. Maybe my brother had simply been hungry enough to finally eat what my grandparents were serving, or perhaps they'd coaxed him just enough with a cleverly devised distraction.

A Winter's Siege

A Play

About the play

This play should come across as a dramatized and somewhat fictional memoir. The piece came to me as I thought about my own family experience, as well as the idea that as we age, we become in many ways like our parents, taking on the hierarchal roles as one generation dies off while another rises to take the place of the patriarchal (or matriarchal) role in the family. In this piece, we have 59-year-old Joseph Kahl coming to visit his aging father. Yet, before he enters the home, he pulls out Shakespeare's Sonnets, a collection of works with which he has had a love-hate relationship throughout most of his academic and professional career. As he aged, growing in both wisdom and experience (though not always maturity as you'll see in the play), his appreciation of the Sonnets grew as well. It is through the wisdom of Shakespeare that he approaches his own memories, seeking to understand each one while still holding on to some of his own youthful cockiness and sarcasm. This scene presents us with Joseph's own issues, both as a teen and as an adult, with the hierarchal order of his family.

CHARACTERS

***(OLD)* Joseph Kahl**

59; teacher of high school English Literature and Drama. He is the play's narrator.

The following characters are played in the past as Joseph Kahl narrates the action, looking back on each scene as a part of his memory.

***(YOUNG)* Joseph Kahl**

19; a younger version, as in memory

Edward Kahl

49; his father.

Willis Kahl

75; Joseph's grandfather and Edward's father. When he speaks, his voice is gruff and much louder than everyone else's. He should come across as generally grumpy.

Paul Kahl

17; Joseph's Brother

David Kahl

45; Joseph's uncle and Edward's brother

SCENE

(OLD JOSEPH enters. He is reading from a book, a complete collection of Shakespeare's sonnets, small enough to fit in his back pocket. It is tattered, suggesting that this is a book he carries with him wherever he goes. Behind him, the framing of a house. This is where the play's action takes place in memory. OLD JOSEPH stops center stage in front of the house.)

OLD JOSEPH:
When forty winters shall besiege thy brow,
And dig deep trenches in thy beauty's field,
Thy youth's proud livery, so gaz'd on now,
Will be a tatter'd weed, of small worth held

(Holding the book up and looking at the audience.)

Ha! Shakespeare's Sonnet 2. I didn't have much of an appreciation for it when I was a teen. When I got to college, I still didn't. Not for his Sonnet's anyway. Though my professors certainly helped to kindle some appreciation for his work in theatre classes. I only hope I can do the same for my own students. I doubt it. At least not in the present. Teenagers: youth's proud livery soon to be nothing more than a tatter'd weed besieged by forty winters. *(Making a sweeping gesture of himself)* Exhibit A.

(He gestures toward the house behind him. It lights up with activity. EDWARD and WILLIS enter. WILLIS is shuffling a deck of cards in his hands. He and EDWARD sit at a card table set up in the living room. DAVID is in the kitchen, busy putting snacks together on a tray.)

Oh. Exhibit B, my father. And Exhibit C, my grandfather. He's dead now. Not in this scene, I mean. But now, in the present. Just so there's no confusion. Dead 30 years ago.

(DAVID exits the kitchen with a tray and enters the living room.)

Oh. Exhibit D, my uncle. My father and uncle, would you believe, are in their mid to late 50s? Good genes. They are still mistaken for being in their 30s. Not sure what happened to me. Must be my healthy regiment of cigars and scotch.

(While the three men at the card table pass around the snacks and sample them, OLD JOSEPH crosses the stage and sits on a bench off to the side of the house. He pulls out a cigar, sniffs it, drawing in its scent. Shrugging his shoulder, he places the cigar in his mouth.)

But enough about me, at least for the present.

(Lights dim on OLD JOSEPH and brighten on the living room.)

WILLIS: *(to EDWARD)* Where's Joey and Paul?

OLD JOSEPH: Joey. I always hated that name. Joe. Joseph. Not Joey.

EDWARD: They'll be here. I told you.

DAVID: *(Laughing. Munching on chips)* You said that fifteen minutes ago.

EDWARD: C'mon. Let's just pass out the cards.

WILLIS: *(Grumbling as he begins to pass out the cards)* Can't even keep a handle on your own kids.

DAVID: Pop. The boys are playing, too. If Ed says they'll be here. They'll be here.

(WILLIS, in mid-pass, glares at DAVID, then at EDWARD. He continues to pass out the cards for three.)

EDWARD: What're you doing?

WILLIS: They're not coming. I told you.

(The game commences)

OLD JOSEPH:
Then being ask'd where all thy beauty lies,
Where all the treasure of thy lusty days

(Musing) Yes. Where? Where were

the treasures of my father's lusty days? I can't remember. *(Smiling)* Probably out hanging with friends. This was winter break right after my first semester of college. *(shuddering)* The holidays. Family obligations. You know how it goes. *(Beat. Turning toward the house)* Ah. Here we are.

(YOUNG JOSEPH and PAUL enter from the front door of the house, which opens into the living room. Quickly, they strip off their winter coats. EDWARD stands and approaches.)

EDWARD: Where've you two been?

YOUNG JOSEPH and **PAUL:** *(Exchanging a glance)* Out. *(They giggle)*

EDWARD: You smell like pot.

OLD JOSEPH: Shit! I forgot about that.

OLD JOSEPH and **YOUNG JOSEPH:** *(Giggling. YOUNG JOSEPH hits PAUL on the shoulder.)* Guilty as charged.

EDWARD: *(Closer, as if to intimidate YOUNG JOSEPH)* Please don't. Not today. Your grandfather's here. *(YOUNG JOSEPH goes complete deadpan)* He's got prostate cancer, you know. So please be kind.

YOUNG JOSEPH: *(Looking at PAUL)* We will.

(EDWARD shifts his gaze and glares at PAUL.)

PAUL: *(Rolls his eyes and lets out a loud sigh)* Geez, dad! Really?

YOUNG JOSEPH: Fine. What're we playing?

EDWARD: Ask your grandfather.

(EDWARD turns, and YOUNG JOSEPH and PAUL follow.)

OLD JOSEPH: You know. It really wasn't my idea. The pot, I mean. It was my brother's. He's the wild one in the family. I only went along because—Well, damn! That shit was really good. But I digress:

To say, within thine own deep sunken eyes,
Were an all-eating shame and thriftless praise.

DAVID: Pop. The boys are here. I told you.

WILLIS: *(Grunting)* I suppose you want to play.

YOUNG JOSEPH: *(Sitting)* Ummm… yeah. Good to see you, grandpa.

WILLIS: *(Waving his hand as if swatting away YOUNG JOSEPH'S remark)* It's Spades. Do you know how to play?

EDWARD: Yeah, pop. They know how to play. We played last—

WILLIS: Will you shut up and let the boy speak?

(Silence. Everyone awkwardly staring at each other while simultaneously avoiding WILLIS'S cold glare.)

YOUNG JOSEPH: *(Realizing all eyes are on him)* Yeah. 13 cards each. We bid tricks. No more than 13 total.

WILLIS: *(Narrowed eyes)* That's right. *(Looking around the table)* We have too many players.

PAUL: It's okay. I'll go.

EDWARD: No. You sit. *(Looking to DAVE)* Dave?

DAVID: *(He has been diving into the snacks this whole time. He realizes he's been asked a question)* Oh. Sure. I'll sit out. Maybe deal.

WILLIS: I'll deal. Joey, you're on my team.

(WILLIS shuffles and deals. Each player grabs his cards, examining them closely until all have been passed out. DAVID should watch and eat with silent amusement in the following.)

WILLIS: Bid.

EDWARD: Five.

YOUNG JOSEPH: Six.

WILLIS: You can't bid six.

YOUNG JOSEPH: Why not?

WILLIS: It only leaves three tricks left.

YOUNG JOSEPH: So...

PAUL: It's okay. I'll bid three. I think I can get three.

WILLIS: *(Pounding the table)* You can't. That's too many.

YOUNG JOSEPH: We can't? Why? Because it's against your rules? Your way of playing?

WILLIS: Don't talk to me about rules. I've been playing this game longer than you've been alive. I've won big in the casino. What have you done?

YOUNG JOSEPH: I… fine… four. What're you bidding on?

WILLIS: *(Growling)* Two.

(The game commences. OLD JOSEPH looks on with amusement. He cuts his cigar.)

OLD JOSEPH: You mind if I smoke? *(Puts the cigar in his mouth, ignites a lighter, and holds it close to the cigar, but not close enough to light it. He puts out the light.)* No. You're right—crowded theatre. Someone's bound to complain. *(Puts away the lighter, but keeps the cigar out, occasionally sucking on the cut end.)* Watch this.

WILLIS: You can't do that!

YOUNG JOSEPH: I told you I'd get six tricks.

WILLIS: *(Throwing the cards down)* game over!

(The players all stare in stunned silence at WILLIS as he gets up)

PAUL: God! This is why I hate playing with him.

EDWARD: *(Following WILLIS into the living room)* C'mon Pop. It's just a game.

OLD JOSEPH: *(with a chuckle)* How much more praise deserv'd thy beauty's use.

DAVID: *(Congratulatory)* Nice work, Joey. He hates to lose.

YOUNG JOSEPH: But we're on the same team. We won this time.

DAVID: *(Grabbing WILLIS'S hand) It* Looks like he had a few tricks still to play.

(EDWARD comes over, leaving WILLIS in the living room. EDWARD stands at the table and stares at YOUNG JOSEPH)

YOUNG JOSEPH and **OLD JOSEPH**: *(Returning EDWARD'S gaze)*

If thou couldn't answer - 'This fair child of mine
Shall sum my count, and make my

old excuse-'

(EDWARD turns and walks into the kitchen. DAVID follows.)

Proving his beauty by succession thine!

(The frame of the house dims to shadows, leaving the scene frozen as if in time.)

OLD JOSEPH: You see, he couldn't. My dad that is. Never a job well done. Nothing.

(The frame of the house dims to black. OLD JOSEPH stands and walks to center stage.)

Which brings us to this point. Like my father before me, I go to make my obligatory visit. But we don't play cards. No. Never cards. His game is Backgammon. Sometimes he wins. Sometimes I do.

(OLD JOSEPH steps into the frame of the house, and the lights come up. EDWARD, much older now, is sitting at the same table with Backgammon open before him. OLD

JOSEPH sits.)

It's your turn, Pop.

(EDWARD grunts. And makes his move. OLD JOSEPH does the same. The game continues in this way as OLD JOSEPH speaks, looking directly at, but not speaking to EDWARD.)

This were to be new-made when thou art old,
And see thy blood warm when thou feel'st it cold.

(end)

III
Youth's Proud Livery

The Caged Bird

A Play

CHARACTERS

NOAH.
Male. 15 years old. Short, compared to CHRISTINA. Plainly attired. Hair disheveled. Glasses that slide down his nose.

CHRISTINA.
Female. 15 years old. Fashionably attired. NOAH's twin sister.

SETTING

At a corner booth in the school cafeteria.

TIME

Present-day. Noon.

SCENE

(At rise, NOAH sitting at a table studying. Enter CHRISTINA with a tray of food. She sits directly next to NOAH and leans in.)

CHRISTINA

Hey. You been here long?

(NOAH continues to read, ignoring her.)

I said -

NOAH

(Without looking up.)

I heard what you said. Now go away.

CHRISTINA

(She periodically crunches into an apple, or carrots, and chews loudly during the next lines of dialogue. NOAH progressively shows signs of irritation.)

But, we're here to study. Whatcha got? Math? Social studies?

NOAH
English. *I Know Why the Caged Bird Sings.*

CHRISTINA
Why?

NOAH
What?

CHRISTINA
Why does the caged bird sing?

NOAH
Maya Angelou. Smart one. Didn't you bring your book?

CHRISTINA
Nah. You brought it. Whatcha doing with it?

NOAH
Annotating. Can you stop chewing so loudly?

CHRISTINA
Yes. But I won't. *(Beat)* Can we study something else? Math, maybe.

NOAH

This is due tomorrow.

CHRISTINA

Then why do it today? I've got a math test after lunch. You have yours tomorrow morning.

NOAH

If we study math, will you stop crunching on your apple?

CHRISTINA

(Takes a big, crunchy bite into her apple, or carrot, and speaks with her mouth full.)

Maybe.

(CHRISTINA crunches. NOAH looks at her.)

Fine.

NOAH

Fine.

(NOAH sets the book to the side and opens the math book.)

Do you want to work on problems one through ten together?

CHRISTINA

Nah. I'll work on this though.

(Grabs the book and stands)

NOAH
Hey! I said I need that!

CHRISTINA
I know. I lost mine.
(Makes to exit.)

NOAH
Yeah. Whatever. I do know why the caged bird sings, by the way.
(Beat)

CHRISTINA
Why?

NOAH
He had a sister like you.

CHRISTINA
Haha. Good one. At least I have this. Great lunch! See ya tonight, Noah.

(CHRISTINA exits.)

NOAH
Oh, for crying out loud. She left her lunch trash. She's so annoying.

(the end)

Unbuttoned

Fiction: Coming of Age

I don't remember when I first saw her. Perhaps it was from afar as I watched her play on the soccer field. Maybe it wasn't. But I was smitten the moment her features met my eyes. She was cuter and far less sexy then. Her curves still showed despite the loose track pants and t-shirts she wore every day. Her outfits had very little variety. I think that's what first drew me to her. Her apparent simplicity.

Impossibly infatuated, I was incapacitated.

You know the feeling when you've been so enthralled by someone that the only thing holding you back and keeping you from talking to that person is sheer terror. Terror at tumbling over your words, at suddenly having nothing to say, or even worse. Committing to a date only to find yourself staring at her from across the table with absolutely nothing to say and still several hours before the date is over.

I first met Michelle. Truly met her, I mean. And not just stared at her from the sidelines or talked to her on the phone after finding out her name and working up the nerve to call her.

We first met at Bible Club, and I wasn't sure if she knew that I was the guy who called her up while she so graciously talked and listened for hours.

But she knew.

I could tell when she came to me and smiled. She was radiant. Her teeth seemed to show whiter and brighter beneath the classroom's fluorescent lights. Her skin, a light brown, blushed. She said hello and barely looked me in the eye. I stammered a hello back to her.

We talked for about a minute, skirting around what we both knew to be truly weird — me getting her number without asking for it and calling her, even though we'd never really met in person.

Maybe she found me in the school yearbook.

Like I found her.

At Bible Club, she got in front of the group and gave her testimony, citing some scripture verses meaningful to her. I was sort of listening. I knew then that I wanted to somehow be a better person. To be someone she would admire as I admired her. For her looks, yes. But also for her kindness and the way she wore a smile and carried herself, inviting everyone into her world.

She was attractive then. Only she didn't know it. Or, perhaps her Protestant morality refrained her from flaunting it. I don't know because I never got a date with her in the ninth grade.

Oh, I'd sit with her at lunch.

A few seats away.

With my band of buddies.

At another table.

I'd look up at her and see her between rolling hills of heads and shoulders that slanted daintily to allow me to catch a glimpse of her as she ate and chatted with her friends.

My buddies, Stephen and Matt. They'd catch me looking at Michelle. One would glance over his shoulder, then back at me. Then, the other would mimic my expression and toss something at my face. Maybe a cold, soggy tater tot would hit its mark, momentarily breaking Michelle's spell on me. I'd come back to my buddies, and they would laugh.

Behind them, nearly back-to-back to Stephen and Matt would be Michelle's friends Eve and Clarisse. Like Stephen and Matt, they were probably staring at Michelle, wondering whose eye she caught when she would smile at me. I'd smile back, which I think would give my friends the perfect opportunity to toss a particle of poorly prepared food in my face. Michelle would cover her mouth with the tips of her fingers, stifling a laugh as her cheeks dimpled and blushed. Eve and Clarisse would glance back at me. And they would roll their eyes.

No matter.

I once worked up the nerve to ask her out.

But I blew it.

I created the moment for casual conversation with Eve and Clarisse when Michelle was not around. Easy to do since they took some honors classes with me while Michelle took, as I would later find out, pretty much all AP courses.

The goal of these conversations was information. I was finding out about Michelle without actually getting to know her. We've all been there, and for me, it was a need. I needed to find that common ground before committing to hours with someone I hardly knew.

She liked the same band as me.

I told her I had two tickets to the show happening that weekend.

"Do you want to come?" I asked.

"Of course," she exclaimed, "that would be awesome!"

So, we had a date, except for one technicality. Did you know that it is not really a date if you do not say 'date' or definitively state 'do you want to go out with me'?

So, there I was — nauseous with

nervousness — and that one simple four-letter word doesn't come out. Instead, it's just an invitation from a friend.

Or acquaintances.

Or strangers.

Two people with endless potential as long as one of them doesn't steer the relationship in the wrong direction or propel it forward too quickly.

"Great," I said as I fought back nausea. "I'll pick you up at your place."

"All right," she said and began to walk with me.

Most guys would be elated by this.

Most guys would even be bold enough to take the girl's hand or maybe put an arm around her waist.

I'm not most guys.

I don't even know what her reaction was when I began to pick up speed. I have a faint memory of her walking beside me and trying to keep up. Maybe she asked if I was okay. But I lost her as I darted into the boy's bathroom and found the last stall. I knelt, taking deep breaths and swallowing until my stomach stopped fluttering.

When I came out of the bathroom, she was gone.

When I saw her again, I didn't bring up the incident.

Neither did she.

She was kind and gracious.

Me, I couldn't wait for our "date."

Here's the thing. There's dating: a guy asks a girl out. Or vice versa. But it's almost always better when the guy asks the question. After that, the girl can say yes or no. It's official and communicates the intention of both parties. Then, they go out. In high school, it's always a little weird, especially if you don't have a car.

"Hey, so, I'll pick you up at 7," you say.

"Great," she says.

Then, you arrive. Your date is all dressed up and smells of strawberries and vanilla. The girl smiles at you, and you smile at her, only you're not looking at her face. You're looking at her cleavage. She notices but doesn't say anything. You bring your eyes up to meet hers. Then, you take her hand in yours and walk her to the car.

Well, your parent's car. A ten-year-old maroon station wagon with some rust around the wheel wells. And this would be all fine and good except that your mom is driving.

Or maybe your dad.

I'm not sure which is worse.

For you, it might be your mom.

For me, it would be my dad. He'd say something weird that would make your date uncomfortable. Then, the two of you would be sitting in the backseat and looking at each other in absolute silence.

You'd wear that expression that says, *I swear I have nothing to do with this.*

She'd wear that expression that says, *Oh, jeez, I'm going out with a loser, who doesn't even have his license.*

And your dad would be sharing these corny jokes and telling these stories about his first date.

And she'd laugh. Not the mocking kind, but the kind that lets you know she's just pleased to be with you. She doesn't think you're a loser. Also, she finds your dad kind of adorable.

At least, that's what Michelle told me when my dad dropped us off at the arena where the band was playing.

"You know," Michelle said as we started to walk, "your dad's kind of cute in that dad sort of way."

"Okay," I said. "Uh… thanks."

She chuckled. "I can see where you get it from." Then, she took my hand and pushed against me a little as we walked.

Silently, I thanked my dad for being my unlikely wingman.

I pulled her closer to me. As close as she could be without knocking me off balance. And we walked like that until we reached the line and she spotted someone she knew. She squealed the way girls sometimes do when they are excited, with the entirety of emotion, shooting like rays of electricity out of their extended fingers. She took off like a rocket.

I thought she was running toward a group of girls, but she passed them as though they didn't exist and ran up to a guy who caught her in his arms and squeezed her one of those big bear hugs. When I caught up to them, he was gently setting her down. Then she, on tiptoes, was giving him a peck on the cheek.

I don't think she saw me.

Or maybe she just didn't notice me on purpose.

Like a puppy placed out in the rain after piddling on the floor, I stood there and waited awkwardly as Michelle and this other guy engaged in a bit of catching up. It wasn't clear if they'd dated previously. It also wasn't clear whether they were just super friendly with each other or whether she just greeted everyone with a 'Holy Kiss.'

Fuck if I knew. This was my first time seeing Michelle outside of school.

"Oh, Brian," Michelle said at last as if I had just arrived. "This is Gabe."

"Hey," I said, trying to play it cool as I took his hand. "How long have you known each other?"

"Oh," Gabe said with eyes that seemed to look past you when he talked. "We kind of grew up together. Michelle's older brother is my best friend."

"Cool," I said, nodding politely as if his response explained everything I needed to know about the history of their relationship.

Meanwhile, Gabe droned on uninterestingly about the older brother I did not know Michelle had. And his incessant talking simply raised more questions. I wondered whether this older brother was also at our high school. If so, should I try to get on this guy's good side? You know, score some points with him and impress little sis. Gabe's monologue did nothing by way of answering any of these unasked questions.

"Anyway," Gabe said at last with an ambiguous wink." You two enjoy the show. I gotta catch up with my girl."

"My brother," Michelle said as she turned to me. "He's a senior."

It took a moment for me to catch up with the knowledge that Gabe would simply not be a contender for Michelle's heart. Then I registered the meaning behind Michelle's comment about her brother.

"Oh," I said dumbly. Then I cleared my throat and added. "My sister's a senior, too."

"Yeah, I know," Michelle said. "We play on the soccer team together. You know, the team you watch when you should be practicing on your field. Anyway, she's… uh… mentioned you before."

"Like what did she say?" I asked, trying to mask my surprise.

Her hazel eyes sparkled. "Like you're a little weird," she said. "Maybe you read too much. But don't worry, I'm a little weird, too. At least that's what my brother says."

We forced a laugh. Mine went on a little longer than hers. She squinted at me as if to say, *The joke's over.*

"Sorry," I said.

"It's okay," Michelle said. She bumped her hip against mine and knocked me off balance. "Happens to the best of us."

We stood in line. Michelle started in on a story of sibling rivalry. I added a similar story when she'd finished. Together, we enjoyed the sweet, safe comfort of friendship. As we talked, we moved forward in the line, getting close enough to each other to rub shoulders. Just close enough so I could casually place my arm around her waist. I took a risk, albeit a small one, in hopes that she would return the gesture.

And she did, placing an arm around my waist. Side by side, we pressed against each other. Warmth resonated from the curve of her hip up to the curve of her breast. My heart raced, simultaneously pumping the heat of longing and desire to my groin and to my head.

Then we separated at the ticket booth,

where I fumbled with my wallet before handing the agent some cash.

"Don't you already have tickets?" Michelle asked.

"I did," I said and fumbled with the rest of my explanation.

Michelle nodded knowingly.

And that night, her physical absence at my side where she had pressed against me for the span of maybe five minutes cooled the heat of my desire. If I'd planned it better, perhaps the night would have ended differently.

Perhaps not.

Nonetheless, we enjoyed the potential of whatever we would be — friends, lovers, gentle companions, the pleasure of our company, or just ships in the night signaling their presence to each other with the flash of lights and the blare of a horn.

In our enjoyment, we watched the show, occasionally stealing a glance at the intriguing mystery who stood to our right or left respectively while the other pretended not to notice.

For two years, I sputtered along in Michelle's wake. I'd steal a glance at her, she'd return my gaze with a smile as she sailed on with a group of her friends. When she'd disappear over the horizon, I'd allow the tide to take me to my next class.

That is, until one afternoon, I was running late. I'd decided upon a shortcut and slammed the release bar to a door that led to a stairwell. It opened to the then unfamiliar sounds of show-tunes.

Michelle and her best friends, Eve and Clarisse, sat on the steps. Their voices were harmonizing, taking full advantage of the acoustics. I tried to walk past them. But a tug at my pant leg held me fast.

"Brian," Michelle sang. "We need a 'Melchior,'" Eve and Clarisse repeated her, as if in a refrain.

"A what?" I asked. I had no idea what she meant. She'd always been a great singer, and we hadn't been hanging out since she'd join the drama club.

In unison, the three of them told me it was for *Spring Awakening*. I still had no idea what the trio meant.

"The musical," they sang. Hot and flirty, chatting in some code known only to themselves, the trio whispered about how perfect I would be.

"Brian," they said. "Sing for us."

So, I did, and my voice cracked until Michelle smiled at me. Two dimpled cheeks, the color of sweet hot cocoa warmed me up to the idea of performing in her show. Though I never sang publicly, I did for her. What guy wouldn't? What with the cute way her smile perked up her cheeks until her hazel eyes sparkled with a wink? Oh, and her boobs that ballooned just slightly out of her tight gingham pattern shirt begging to be unbuttoned.

Boy, had she grown.

She snagged me like a ship run aground on a coral reef.

Caught in the throes of raging hormones that overcame any sense I had — I had none. If I did, I would have hoisted my sails and retreated like an outgunned ship until the predatory danger of involving myself with a girl I knew was now way above my league found some other hapless victim.

Like most theatre girls in high school, she had about her an intriguing mystery magnified by every *too-tight-in-just-the-right-places* outfit she wore. They were tight enough to cause a guy to stumble up steps as he did a double-take. He'd watch her descend a crowded stairwell between classes. That's when she'd glance over her shoulder and flash the guy a rosy smile.

Yeah, it was definitely her smile that had me.

"Brian," Michelle sang sweetly. "Come perform in our play."

"I don't know, maybe," I told her.

"But you'll be great," Eve and Clarisse chimed in, adding some mindless laughter of their own.

"When?" I asked them.

"Here," Michelle said. She stood up with a bounce and waved a form in front of me.

Being just out of my reach, I stepped closer the way sailors hypnotized by the siren's song sail closer to land until they shipwreck. Even then, they don't realize it. Neither did I, not with the scent of strawberries and vanilla wafting toward me, drawing me closer until I landed upon her island, and I was trapped.

So, yeah. I unbuttoned her…

Curiosity.

And she led me down territory that my seventeen years would have never led me on their own. We performed. On stage, that is. And we became that weird mismatched theatre couple. Me, the guy who grew to the underwhelming height of 5-foot-9. She, the girl whose bosoms blossomed beyond a B in middle school and surpassed a D in high school. I'm only guessing, though. I never bothered to understand bra sizes. But, still, you get the point.

And the point is this. A girl's charming smile and her self-confidence will get a guy to do just about anything.

Timothy R. Baldwin

A Bazaar Christmas

Fiction: Cozy Mystery/Young Adult

Garland and lights hung from the gymnasium walls and the smell of nutmeg and cinnamon filled the air. The static of old speakers churned out Christmas music while vendors packed their wares — crafts, treats, and other homemade items. Meanwhile, lingering shoppers, their arms already loaded down with goods, seemed to pester vendors for that final sale of the night. My mom was one such vendor. As with years past, she wasted no time to pack up.

"Marcus, help me with this," Mom said as she knelt behind one of the many tables lining the school gymnasium.

"Sure," I said, kneeling opposite her to assist with a crate.

On the count of three, Mom and I grunted as we lifted and placed the crate on the table.

"I thought you'd sell out of scrapbook material," I said. "It looks like you're coming home with twice as much."

Mom scowled. "It's actually half." She added a wink. "There might be something in there for you and Bri."

"Thanks, Mom," I said. "I'm going to go see if any of the other vendors need help."

There was still so much to do to close out the annual Christmas Bazaar. As the son of the longest-running PTSA president and the son of the assistant principal, everyone came to expect that I'd be around to help out at every event.

I didn't mind helping out, especially since I was in good company who I spotted coming toward us. My girlfriend, Alissa, carried a stack of cardboard boxes as she trailed a few paces behind her mother, Mrs. Claude.

I waved. "Hey. Can I give you a hand?"

Alissa grinned. "You bet! Here."

She handed me the entire stack, which I fumbled as I turned, letting several flattened boxes slide off the top of the stack and onto the table.

"Jeez! These are heavy," I said.

She placed a hand on her hip. "Glad you finally admitted it. I'm stronger."

On the other side of the table, Mom and Mrs. Claude laughed.

Before I could give a comeback, shouting from the other side of the gymnasium drew my attention. A group of patrons circled around the silent auction table, creating a din that echoed throughout the gymnasium. Other vendors, parents and their kids, stopped their packing to have a look.

"Oh dear," Mom said. "We should go put out that fire."

Mom and Mrs. Claude jogged over to the crowd. Alissa and I followed close behind.

As we drew near, a middle-aged man dressed in a tweed jacket and a Santa hat stood on a chair.

"If you would please all take a moment," he said. "I'm sure we can sort this out."

"Hey!" A stout balding man roared. "What kind of a place are you running here?"

Mom stepped in. "Mr. Robinson. Please step down. And you, sir —"

"Johnston Hill," the stout balding man said, stepping close to Mom. She stepped back, her eyes darting around.

Mrs. Claude stepped in. "You'd do well to back up, Mr. Hill."

Mr. Hill pointed at Mr. Robinson. "This guy here in the tweed says the grand prize TV I won in the silent auction is missing."

Mr. Robinson stepped off the chair. "Easy now. I returned only moments ago. When I'd left, it was here. I'm sure it was just misplaced."

"Just like last year," someone said.

"Last year?" a booming voice spoke up. We turned to see a bearded man in a football jersey. "Are you talking about the stereo system that went missing?"

"No, that was the year before," another person corrected. Others chimed in, arguing about what went missing when.

"What are they talking about?" Mr. Hill said. He spun. "Mr. Robinson, you..."

Mr. Hill's voice trailed off. The chair once occupied by Mr. Robinson was empty.

Mr. Hill pulled out a handkerchief and wiped his brow. "I need to speak to whoever's in charge. Who would that be?"

Mom stepped up to Mr. Hill. "That'll be me. I'm sure we can —"

"You better hope you do, because —"

"Sir," Mom said. "Why don't you step over here with us while the others finish picking up their items?"

I glanced at Alissa. "Where'd Mr. Robinson go?"

Alissa shrugged. "Every time I stopped by this table, he had a mouth full of roasted walnuts. Maybe it caught up to him."

We laughed.

Mrs. Claude marched over to us. "Alissa Imani Claude, I don't know what you think is so funny. There's a TV missing." She glared at me. "And Marcus, your mother is trying to placate an angry patron."

"Sorry," Alissa and I said.

Mrs. Claude held up a hand. "Marcus, we need you to go find your father. After that, we need you both to look for the TV."

"On it!" Alissa said. "C'mon, Marcus."

Once in the hallway, Alissa pulled me off to the side. "You realize what'll happen if that TV isn't recovered."

I nodded. "Another lost item and we won't have a Bazaar next year."

"Which means fewer funds in the booster clubs," Alissa said. "Once we find your father, we're gonna find that TV and whoever took it."

"I propose we start with Mr. Robinson," I said. "He dipped out a little too quick."

Alissa grinned. "Sounds like a plan!"

We jogged down the hallway, passing a man in a red flannel who called out. "You two stop running!"

We ignored him as we hooked a right at the next intersection. Once around the corner, we came to the glassed-in main office. Dad, dressed in khakis and a holiday tie, stood at the counter counting cash with Ms. Berry, one of our math teachers.

Dad and Ms. Berry looked up when Alissa and I entered.

"You two can't be here," Dad said.

"We've got a problem in the gymnasium," Alissa said.

"It'll have to wait," Dad said.

"It can't!" I insisted. "Mom is trying to calm a Mr. Hill who —"

"Oh brother!" Ms. Berry said. "Mr. Kahale, you'll want to handle this one quickly."

Dad turned to us. "What's the problem?"

Alissa and I started talking at the same time about the missing TV.

Dad held up a hand. "Alright. Alright. I'll take care of it. Uh… Ms. Berry. Let me lock this up and we'll get back to it shortly."

Ms. Berry placed the cash and receipts in the lockbox and handed it to Dad. With the lockbox in hand, Dad disappeared into the office.

Folding her arms across her chest, Ms. Berry leaned on the counter. "The school really can't afford to lose that TV. If you know what I mean."

Dad returned before Alissa and I could say anything else. "What're you all standing around for? Let's go!"

Allissa and I followed as Dad led the charge back toward the gymnasium. Ms. Berry remained two strides behind him. When they rounded a corner, Alissa and I stopped.

Alissa turned to me. "We need to find Mr. Robinson, and fast!"

"What do you have in mind? I asked.

Alissa grinned. "Follow my lead."

In the gymnasium, Dad and Ms. Berry had taken Mr. Hill to the side. Though the man no longer hollered at everyone who happened to pass by, he gritted his teeth as he wrung his handkerchief in his hands.

Alissa and I took the center of the gymnasium where we caught a cold draft sweeping through the great room. Alissa hugged herself as we surveyed the room. Under Mom's direction, volunteers had already begun to take down garland and tinsel, while vendors continued to pack things away. The bearded man wearing the football jersey seemed to bounce between tables, talking loudly about sports and the trips he had planned for the holiday break. A woman carrying a few smaller bags seemed to hug the bleachers as she trekked across the gymnasium.

"Have you spotted Mr. Robinson?"

Alissa asked.

"No," I said. "So, let's not rule him out."

Alissa nodded. "Until then, who else looks like they could've swiped a big screen TV?"

"Let's see," I replied as a I rubbed my chin. "It's kind of bulky and weighs at least a hundred pounds. Maybe football jersey over there."

Alissa shrugged. "Maybe. Wait!" She grabbed my shoulder. "Do you see that guy over there? He was in the hallway when we went to get your father."

On the far side of the gymnasium, a man in jeans and a red flannel kept his eyes to the floor. He headed straight toward the auxiliary gym.

"Isn't there a back entrance somewhere over there?" I asked.

"Yeah!" Alissa said. "Let's follow, but not too close."

We ducked behind a small cluster of people packing things away at the nearest table. Keeping ourselves close to the wall, we made our way toward the auxiliary gym. When the wall cornered off, Alissa peeked beyond it.

She turned back to me. "He's not there, but there is a wide-open door at the other end."

With one last look around the gymnasium, we confirmed no one noticed what we were up to. While Dad remained with Mr. Hill, Mom seemed to be directing patrons out the doors so vendors could finish packing. Mrs. Claude had moved on to assist with further clean-up. Mr. Robinson still hadn't shown. Alissa and I exchanged a quick nod and slipped around the corner.

Wads of unused garland and assorted boxes of green and red looked out of place next to the gym equipment scattered in stations around the room. On the far side of the room, a water fountain trickled onto the floor. By its side, an open steel door.

"Shall we?" Alissa asked.

Something beyond the open door rattled. Alissa grabbed my hand. We waited, listening to the trickle of water.

"I think we're good," Alissa said. "Stay close."

When we reached the door, we took a peek inside the room. Mechanical equipment lined one wall. The room also housed stacks of boxes, a broken cart, and an old Christmas tree.

"It's just a utility closet," I said.

"Figures," Alissa said. "I've been dying to dive into another mystery."

I sighed. "Me, too. We should go."

As we turned to leave, a grunt followed by a heavy crash came from above. A ladder mounted on the wall led into an open access door in the ceiling.

"Do you think…" I grabbed a rung and lifted myself up.

Alissa pulled me back. "Marcus, you can't go up there!"

"Why not?" I asked. "That's a perfect place to hide a TV."

She crossed her arms. "Sure. And one guy is going to lift it up there and squeeze it through just to take it out when everyone's gone."

"What about two guys?" I asked.

"Who's down there?" A man called from above. Heavy footsteps made their way from one side of the ceiling to the other. In the opening of the ceiling, a face appeared. "What do you two need?"

That's when I recognized the head custodian. "Uh, sorry Mr. Ford. We were looking for—"

"Sorry to bother you," Alissa said, pulling me away.

With that false lead out of the way, Alissa and I squirreled ourselves into a corner of the gymnasium far away from the utility closet. Hidden away, we took that moment to survey what remained of the bazaar. Mom directed a group of volunteers to break down the empty tables. Football jersey was among those volunteers helping with Mom. Meanwhile, Mrs. Claude remained by the silent auction table as winners picked up the few remaining items. A few feet away from her, Mr. Hill sat wiping his forehead and glaring at every person who passed by him, as if he suspected everyone of taking off with the TV. Dad and Ms. Berry weren't around.

"What next?" Alissa asked.

"Not sure," I said. "Still no sign of Mr. Robinson."

"Any idea what he drives?" Alissa asked. "Maybe we could check the parking lot."

"Let's go ask my mom," I said.

As we made our way over to Mom, Mr. Ford entered the main gymnasium. He spotted Mom and approached her. After talking briefly, she pointed toward the main office.

"Well, your mother definitely knows something," Alissa said.

"Put those tables and chairs in the corner," Mom said, directing her comments toward a couple of tired-looking fathers. They complied. Mom turned to us as we approached.

"Where've you two been?" She asked. "Wait. Let me guess. Following Mr. Ford around."

I cringed. "Oops."

"Uh-huh," Mom said. "Your father asked Mr. Ford to check the wiring. It seems the security cameras are fried."

Alissa and I exchanged a glance. "Do you think?"

Mom laughed. "Don't be silly. No one cut the wires so they could steal a TV."

I muttered. "Hearing you say it like that…"

"Makes it sound pretty stupid," Alissa finished.

Mom smiled. "Don't worry about it. I'm sure it'll turn up."

"Hey," Alissa said. "Has Mr.

Robinson returned? He was the last person to see it, right?"

"Probably," Mom said. "But I haven't seen him since Mr. Hill had a fit."

"What does his car look like?" I asked. "Maybe we could —"

A loud crash cut me off. Mom spun. "You've got to be kidding."

A pile of tables lay scattered across the floor next to the wall. Two men, their shoulders slumped, stood several feet away from the tables. As Mom headed over to the pair, she called over a few others to help out, leaving Alissa and me alone.

Alissa turned toward the auction table. "We should've started with Mr. Robinson."

"Well he couldn't have gotten far," I said. "Wait! Where did football jersey go?"

"There he is!" Alissa pointed. The man had his phone up to his ear as he headed in the direction of the auction table.

Alissa and I ran after him. Before I could catch up to football jersey, my shin collided with a metal object and I collapsed on the floor. Alissa skidded to a halt. As I rose, I took in the handcart, the jeans, and the red flannel.

Mr. Ford set the hand truck down and glared at us. "First you're running in the hallways. Then you're snooping in the utility closets. What are you kids up to?"

"We're sorry," Alissa said, helping me up.

"I'm really sorry, Mr. Ford," I said, cringing as I favored my right leg.

Mr. Ford looked around the gymnasium. "Look at this mess. Every year the PTSA holds this bazaar, and every year things are left out of place. It's late and the shift is almost over. Now someone needs a hand truck to move some big-screen TV."

"Mr. Ford, do you know where the TV is?" Alissa asked.

He scowled. "Now why would I know where that is. Do I look like Best Buy or something?"

I choked back a laugh. For a second, Mr. Ford glared at me until his glare transformed into a grin.

"Doesn't matter," Mr. Ford said. "It looks like you two know more about this TV than I do. Why don't I leave this hand truck with you? Put it in the utility closet when you're done."

"Yes, sir," Alissa said.

When I didn't respond, Alissa pushed me lightly on the shoulder.

"I... sorry again for running into you," I said.

"Don't worry about it," Mr. Ford said.

Armed with a hand truck, I thought about Mr. Robinson's casual remark about the TV being misplaced.

Alissa grabbed the hand truck and tipped it on an angle. "Well, let's not just stand here."

"Wait," I said. "You remember what football jersey's said about the missing stereo system?"

Alissa let go of the hand truck. "Where're you going with this?"

"Lis, don't you see?" I asked.

She nodded slowly. "You're thinking it was a distraction. It's circumstantial, but that's about the time Mr. Robinson disappeared."

"Now football jersey is gone," I said. "I betcha he was talking to Mr. Robinson on the phone."

Alissa crossed her arms. "Now you're stretching it. Besides —" She crinkled her nose as the scent of something stale and smokey wafted through the gymnasium. "What's that smell?"

"I think it's coming from over there," I said, pointing toward the silent auction table. "The side door is probably open."

Alissa took the lead as we ran toward the side door.

"Alissa!" Mrs. Claude called.

Alissa and I halted.

"Mom! We need to hurry. There's someone —"

"Let's go then." Mrs. Claude grabbed her jacket and led the way outside as she put it on.

Once outside, we were greeted by a light snow fall and the distinct smell of cigarette smoke clinging in the damp air. To our left, football jersey paced the loading dock, talking on the phone and puffing on a cigarette. On the edge of the loading dock sat a large object draped in a tarp. Alissa and I followed Mrs. Claude as she approached the loading dock.

"Excuse me, sir," Mrs. Claude said. "You can't smoke here."

Football jersey turned. "Sorry, I didn't know." He dropped his cigarette and stomped on it. "I'm about ready to go. Waiting on my friend to pull up."

Mrs. Claude nodded. "What's under the tarp?"

"This?" Football jersey asked. He stepped toward the tarped object. "It was here when I came outside."

Mrs. Claude closed the distance between her and football jersey, beating him to the tarped object. Despite his size, football jersey took a step back as Mrs. Claude lifted the tarp. She turned to us. "Can you two go tell Mr. Hill his TV is waiting for him? After that, please return the hand truck."

"On it!" We both said.

As we headed inside, I heard Mrs. Claude say, "I'm sure glad you were here keeping an eye on this."

Once inside, we made our first stop where Mr. Hill sat with his arms crossed.

"Excuse me, Mr. Hill," Alissa said. "My mother is waiting by the loading dock with your TV. Someone must've put it there for you to pick up."

Mr. Hill stood. "You've got to be kidding me!"

As Mr. Hill hobbled away, I realized Mr. Robinson hadn't returned.

"What if Mr. Robinson was pulling his vehicle up to the loading dock?" I asked.

"Doesn't matter now," Alissa said. She hooked her arm into mine. "Let's go help your mother. She'll be glad to know we found the TV."

We found Mom struggling with the tables that had toppled onto the floor. "Oh good," Mom said. "You two came just in the nick of time. The guys who were helping me had to leave."

"We can help," I said. "You'll also want to know Mr. Hill is far happier now that he has his TV."

"Oh good," Mom said. "Where was it?"

"It was on the loading dock," Alissa said.

"Well," Mom said. "Let's sort the rest of this stuff out so the custodial staff can get out of here on time."

Just then, a flustered Mr. Robinson joined us. "Mrs. Kahale. I'm sorry, I looked everywhere. The TV is gone."

"No, it's not," Mom said. "Mystery solved. And you have our two detectives here to thank."

Mr. Robinson shot us a wide-eyed look. "That's… great! Where was it?"

"It was sitting on the loading dock under a tarp," Alissa said.

"That's bizarre," Mr. Robinson said. "It was…" As he fumbled around for the right words, I noticed dampness on the shoulders of his tweed jacket.

"Where were you anyway?" I asked.

"Here's the thing," Mr. Robinson said. "I… there was… an emergency and —"

"That's okay," Mom said. "We don't need to hear anymore. But since you're here, why don't you help us with these tables."

Alissa and I took either side of a table and exchanged a glance. Something about Mr. Robinson didn't add up. In the process of recovering the TV, I suspected we also discovered the source of several other missing items. We couldn't prove anything, yet. But we ensured there would be another Christmas Bazaar. If Mr. Robinson tried anything in the future, we'd be watching, especially if football jersey showed up.

Vitality

A Play

CHARACTERS

NOAH.
15. Plainly dressed. Hair disheveled. Glasses that slide down his nose. Played with a shy stubbornness.

JANICE.
17. Extravagantly dressed. Hair and make-up done up. School socialite.

SETTING

A school hallway. F. Scott Fitzgerald High School. An inspirational statement reads, "Vitality shows in not only the ability to persist but the ability to start over." To the right of the sign is an analogue clock set to 2:44. It ticks continuously throughout the scene.

TIME

Present day. After school.

SCENE

(At rising an analog clock mounted on the wall ticks away. A school bell rings, followed by the unseen chatter of students at the end of a school day.)

(Chatter fades as JANICE enters. She stops and looks around before sitting on the bench. She takes out a binder and a book from her backpack and begins to flip through its pages.)

(NOAH enters. He sees JANICE, clears his throat, and waves. JANICE doesn't see him. He repeats this action, then turns to exit.)

JANICE
Noah, hey!

NOAH
Oh. Hey! I was just…

JANICE
Leaving.

NOAH
No. I. Yeah.

JANICE
In class, you seemed happy to study together.

NOAH
About that…

JANICE
Are you?

NOAH
Am I?
(beat)
Yes. Of course. Why wouldn't I be?

JANICE
I don't know. You seem off. Did you forget-

NOAH
No.
(Taking off his bag and rummaging through it.)
I… uh… have them. Right here.
(He pulls out a copy of The Great Gatsby and a notebook.)

JANICE

(Waving her copy and a notebook.)

Great! Because you know I have mine.

NOAH

(As he approaches JANICE.)

I was wondering. Do you…

JANICE

Why don't you sit? Kinda hard to work together if you're standing.

NOAH

(Sits)

So, do you want… to begin.

JANICE

Sure. Ummm… page?

NOAH

…

JANICE

Did you hear me?

NOAH

Oh. Yeah.

JANICE
Well? What page should we start on?

NOAH
(flipping through a notebook.)
Our essay tomorrow. It covers chapters one through five. So we should probably start somewhere within there.

JANICE
Yeah. Thanks. I kinda figured that.
(beat)
So. What did you think about chapter five?

NOAH
(Off guard)
What? Like with Nick? Daisy? Gatsby?

JANICE
Yeah.
(Imitating)
Like. All of it.

NOAH
(Flips through his notes. They are clearly full.)
Well. It's interesting really. The chapter begins with Nick's house. Like

it's on fire. Unreal. But it's actually Gatsby's house.

(JANICE begins to scribbly copiously as NOAH continues.)

Then, there's not a sound. Even though all the lights are on. It's like there's no life. The wind is blowing and making the lights go off and on. It says, "as if the house had winked into the darkness". Then the taxi. It groans away. The scene begins. Real-

(Seeing JANICE writing every word he says.)

Hey. You're just copying.

JANICE
Am not.

NOAH
You are. Did you even read the chapter?

JANICE
I did. I mean. I read a summary.
(beat)
On Sparknotes.

NOAH
You can't just... You know... Mr. Boyd. He'll know that you just read... that.

JANICE
He doesn't read all of our essays.

NOAH
He does. And I don't want you to...

JANICE
To?

NOAH
Fail.

JANICE
Then help me.

NOAH
(miserably)
Okay. How about we begin-

JANICE
Here.

NOAH
(Pointing at a page in his book)
Here? Right here?

JANICE

(Leaning in. Places a finger on a section in NOAH's copy)

Right here. "Are you in love with me," she said low in my ear. "Or why did I have to come alone?" They're like, cousins, or something, right? So, they'd have to meet alone. Because it would be scandalous. You know.

NOAH

(Quietly)

No... No I don't know. That's not why they-

(Louder)

Maybe we should...

(Clears his throat. Louder. Mustering confidence.)

You know. Get together, or something. And, you know. Talk about this.

JANICE

(put off)

What? Aren't we doing that right now?

NOAH

Yes. Sorry. I meant.... This was a terrible mistake. I shouldn't have... come.

JANICE

You're acting weird. Weirder than normal.

NOAH

Did my sister put you up to this?

JANICE

To what? I just need to pass this test. And I thought you'd

(NOAH and JANICE speak their next lines simultaneously.)

JANICE

Help me study.

NOAH

Give you the answers.

JANICE

No.

NOAH

Oh.

TOGETHER
Can we-
(beat)

NOAH
Start over?

JANICE
Sure. I mean. If you want to?

NOAH
I do.
(beat)
"We've met before."
(an abortive laugh)

JANICE
(beat)
I don't get it. We've known each other since we were. What? Five, or something?

NOAH
No. Yeah. I mean. It's from the book. Gatsby gets Nick to set up a meeting between himself and Daisy. Only, he wants it to appear completely coincidental. So, Gatsby says this to Nick about him and Daisy. Only, he is really uncomfortable. Like, he's not

really good at… You know?

JANICE
(Faint smile. Understanding.)
Yeah. I think I do.
(Flipping through the pages)
Like what you say when you don't know what else to say.

NOAH
Something like that.

(There is an extended pause. JANICE pulls at NOAH's notebook. NOAH snatches at it, but he is too slow.)

(With the following lines: JANICE gets up and reads silently as she walks away. He tries to get it back, but JANICE pulls it away. The following lines and choice of corresponding physical action should communicate a keep-away game.)

NOAH
You can't have that.

JANICE
Why not? I'm just trying to read it.

NOAH
Well. You can't. You have to read the book.

JANICE
I've read the book.

NOAH
Not enough.

JANICE
Enough. And this will help me read it more.

NOAH
Please give it back.

JANICE
Why?

NOAH
Because you have to do your own work, and-

JANICE
(Holds up a page. Scrawled on the page is her name outlined with a heart)
What's this?

NOAH
It's… I…

JANICE
Oh. Noah. Honey. You don't -

NOAH
(quickly)
My sister. She drew that.

JANICE
Christina? I don't think so. This isn't her handwriting.

NOAH
Can I just have my notes back?

JANICE
But I need them.

NOAH
No. You. Don't. I need them.
(beat)

JANICE
Did you draw this?

NOAH
Yes.

JANICE
...

NOAH
(Sigh. Resignation.)
I like you.

JANICE
Okay.

NOAH
Just okay?

JANICE
What do you want me to say? I like you back, or something?

NOAH
Well?

JANICE
Well. You're like a little brother to me. A very weird little brother. And, of course, I like you. But not like that.

NOAH
But I see you. Waving and smiling at me from across the cafeteria. You even come to sit with me. And leave your boyfriend—

JANICE
My boyfriend?

NOAH
Yeah. Trevor, I think?

JANICE
Trevor? He is definitely not my boyfriend.

NOAH
(*Hopeful)*
No?

JANICE
No. I mean… Yeah, I like him. But, he's just a friend.

NOAH
So, you're not seeing anyone?

JANICE
…

NOAH
Janice? You're not—

JANICE
NO!
(Beat)
Sorry. I didn't mean to-

NOAH
It's okay.

JANICE
Can we sit?
(Beat. JANICE sits. Gestures for NOAH to do the same. He does. A large space between NOAH and JANICE on the bench.)
Look. Let's say we were to... you know... date. Hypothetically, I mean. It would change—

NOAH
I know. You might not be Miss Popular anymore because of-

JANICE
Yes. What?! No. That's not what I mean.
(Beat)
Look. Why are you so... into me?

NOAH
I don't...

(shrugs)

I mean. I do. It's hard to... You're always so kind to me. Since we were kids. Do you remember when you used to go camping with us?

JANICE

Yeah.

(Pleasant reminiscence)

A whole week with you... With your family. I always looked forward to that.

NOAH

(quietly)

Me too. Not for the camping. I hate camping. But because you would be there.

JANICE

Oh.

(slow realization)

For how long?

NOAH

All week.

JANICE

No. How long have you... liked me... like this.

NOAH

Since… You remember the time I got lost in the woods? We were seven. And you—

JANICE

Christina and I found you. You had slipped and fallen down a crevice in the rocks and-

NOAH

And you climbed down and stayed with me while my sister went and got help.

JANICE

You were hurt and crying. I couldn't just—

NOAH

You held me.

JANICE

Because you—

NOAH

You smelled like pine and—

JANICE

Those were the trees. We were in

the—

NOAH
And lavender.

JANICE
Oh. I didn't—

NOAH
You still do. I mean. Smell like lavender.

JANICE
...

NOAH
I—

JANICE
Noah. Please don't.

NOAH
I just wanted to ask—

JANICE
(Shoving notebook into NOAH's chest)
Here. You can have your notes back.

(Extended pause.)

(JANICE grabs her things, turns, and walks quickly toward the exit)

NOAH
Janice.
(JANICE stops.)
I'm sorry. I really screwed this up.

JANICE
You… I… it's okay. Don't worry about it.

NOAH
Do you want to… you know… still study together?

JANICE
(Hesitation.)
Like. Right now?

NOAH
Yes. Or, another time.

JANICE
I think.
(Smiling)
That would be nice.

NOAH
Okay. Great!

(NOAH gathers up his things.)

JANICE

Great.

(Exiting. Stops. Flips open her notebook. Writes something on a blank sheet and tears it out.)

Hey, Noah.

(NOAH looks up.)

Here's my number. Text me will you?

NOAH

Thanks. You're not going to… you know… tell Christina about this. Are you?

JANICE

Seriously?

(NOAH nods)

God, no!

(Laughs)

Can you imagine what she would say?

NOAH

I can.

(Beat)

So… see you around?

JANICE
Of course.

(JANICE exits)

(NOAH watches her leave. He sits and looks at the piece of paper in his hands. Then he looks up, filled with pleasure and confusion.)

(Fade to black.)

(end)

IV
Pleasure and Confusion

A Heretical Guide to Classifying Beer

Creative Nonfiction: Satire

If you have friends like mine, you're bound to wind up at some holiday party this year. At those parties, someone will likely encourage you to try the latest beer by a local microbrewery. Your friends will grin with enthusiasm, saying, "You've got to try this." And you'll drink out of a community cup like it's a Christmas Eve service, only no one will feign sanitizing its rim by wiping it with a white cloth. Simultaneously, your friends will boastfully proclaim the gospel of beer, using words like aromatic, assertive, or complex. You'll take them at their word, and maybe you'll agree with your friends, or perhaps you'll know instantly they're as ignorant about beer as you are. But, only if you're honest.

Growing up, I didn't know much about beer, and I can't say that I know a lot about it now. But if I did know more, I could talk to you about beer being ingrained in cultures worldwide since Noah's Ark, with the earliest recorded recipes dating back to 4300 BC. I could talk to you about how the ancient Egyptians brewed beer commercially and had various social traditions associated with beer, such as an Egyptian gentleman offering a lady a sip of his beer, thus announcing their betrothal. I could also talk to you about how the early brewers used balsam, hay, dandelion, and even crab claw for flavoring. I could even go into detail about beer's various uses during the Medieval period beyond its use for nutrition and celebration. These include tithing, trading, payment, and even taxing.

Furthermore, I could go into some depth about the addition of hops to the brewing process in 1000 AD and how 200 years later, it became a substantial commercial enterprise in Eastern Europe. I could even share some very fun facts like how kings used beer to toast victories and how Queen Elizabeth I of England drank strong ale for breakfast. Furthermore, in the colonial period, George Washington and Thomas Jefferson each had their private brewhouses. Then, as the discussion looms upon modern history, I could even go into some depth about how before the 1800s, most beers were simply some variation of ale. And, of course, Louis Pasteur's discovery of yeast in 1876 significantly impacted the fermentation process for beer (and wine), thus leading to over 2300 breweries in the U.S. in 1880 and Pabst's ability, alone, to brew 1 million barrels in a year. But, I won't go into these fun historical facts because this information is easily accessible on beerhistory.com. Here, in addition to a concise timeline, one can find a list of well over twenty books and articles on this very topic.

If beer were a religion, it would probably be the oldest religion in the world, with various offshoots and sects preferring barley over wheat, hoppier beers versus sweeter beers, light beers over dark beers, stouts or porters over ales and lagers, and so forth. If beer were a religion, then the prophets of this religion, who describe their beers with terms like "sessionable" and "malt-driven" and enthusiastically proclaim their beer as "having a balanced interplay between malt and hop bitterness," would cry heresy. Furthermore, they'd burn me at the stake for refusing to adhere to their strict standards of description, all of which you can find on the Beer Style Guide at craftbeer.com.

Now, in my earlier years as a beer novice, I would have given a person a blank stare at the mention of such phrases. Though I don't anymore, not because I lay claim to any actual expert knowledge on the matter. Instead, I've experimented with various beers, mostly at parties that are just as much about trying new and exciting beers as they are about meeting new and exciting people. As a result, I've come to conclude that beers, regardless of the family in which they fall (i.e. lager, pale ale, brown ale, stout, porter, and so forth), are like people you might meet at a party. They can fit into the following categories: *The Eccentric, The Nice Guy/Gal, The Life of the Party,* and *The Asshole.* Hence, the almost heretical way in which I intend to set out to describe beer. I will purposefully move away from any terminology that demands some technical expertise into this world by describing beer in terms that would be more accessible to the ordinary individual. Technical language, I think, will only inhibit one's enjoyment of beer, as opposed to enhancing the experience. Therefore, I will categorize beer as follows: the Eccentric, the Nice Guy / Gal, The Life of the Party, and the Asshole. When experiencing beer within each of these categories, one might boldly proclaim *Another Round, I'll Drink it if There's Nothing Else,* or *Hell no!*

To demonstrate this thesis, I chose Sierra Nevada's Beer Camp Across the World, a collection of collaborative projects containing twelve different kinds of beers. For the sake of brevity and to eliminate redundancy, I have chosen four of these twelve beers to illustrate how these categories might work for the average beer drinker.

The Eccentric. Simultaneously intriguing and off-putting, the West Coast Style DIPA gives off an aroma almost identical to peeling a grapefruit. However, upon taking your first sip, you experience bursts of sweet citrus in the same way you would if you were biting into a slice of tangerine. The sweetness lingers for a brief moment before it's overwhelmed by the taste of sour grapefruit, causing your eyes to squint and your lips to pucker. Upon swallowing, the aftertaste is bitter but not unbearable. This beer is very much like the eccentric person you'd meet at a party. These people hold your attention until the conversation begins to lag or veers into topics in which you have no interest. You wonder whether this West Coast Style DIPA, boasting of 8.3% alcohol, is something you can, or even should, actually finish. But finish it you do because it feels like such a waste, this far into the pint, to stop. Not only that, but you have no one else to pass it off to, and you feel bad about leaving it alone. To this beer, you might say, "Eh… I'll drink it again if there is nothing else around."

The Nice Guy/Gal. The Dunkle Weiss, a German-Bavarian style beer, tries very hard to be well-liked. It is neither inoffensive nor off-putting. With 5.7% alcohol, this beer smells like a fresh spring breeze across a field of grass sprinkled with patches of newly blossoming flowers. Upon your first sip, you are greeted by the familiar taste of cherry candies, like the ones the old ladies at church carry in their purses. Molasses, mild and watered down, are also noticeable within your first few sips. As you continue to drink this beer, you will even notice hints of cocoa powder, like the air you breathe in through your mouth while pouring hot cocoa mix into a dry mug. Hot cocoa powder is the mild chocolaty finish you get upon swallowing your first sip and every sip after that. Like the Nice Guy or Gal at the party, everyone spends some time with this beer. Some, like myself, will ask for another round, while others are content with the experience of just one. However, you will go back to this beer at some point because it is a delightful drinking experience.

The Life of the Party. If the nice guy or gal should suddenly develop charisma, this person would become the one who makes everyone laugh yet does so in a way that offends no one at all. The Atlantic Style Vintage Ale is one such beer. Upon giving it an introductory sniff, a faint plummy aroma wafts through your nostrils, much like the mist of body spray from five feet away. Upon your first sip, fruit punch greets your pallet, taking you back to your childhood, where you sit on the back stoop in the hot sun, sipping through a straw-stuffed into a box of juice. It's pleasant. Yet, there is a mild bitterness to this fruit punch taste that enhances rather than overwhelms the experience. It is much like the taste of tonic water added to the bowl of fruit punch to liven up the drink at a dry party. With its 8.5% alcohol per volume, this beer one that everyone at the party will likely want to drink because the taste is truly something to be experienced. Partygoers everywhere will elevate the harbinger of this experience to the same exalted level of

"Life of the Party," even if he or she didn't supply the beer. Because of the higher alcohol content and the taste of this beer, I would say, "Another round!"

The Asshole. The Dry Hopped Barley Wine Style Ale clothes itself with the appearance of The Eccentric. The asshole has opinions. It makes various and unfounded claims, all of which are initially intriguing, but the more you are around the asshole, the more uncomfortable you feel due to the asshole having complete disregard for anyone but himself. This beer gives off the sweet, citrusy aroma of orange blossoms, and you think, "Yeah! This is gonna be great!" However, when you sip it for the first time, you are reminded of that one time when you insufficiently peeled an orange and suffered the bitter consequences of chewing the remnants of said peel. However, the sweet citrus taste initially offsets the bitterness by leaving you with the aftertaste you get when you eat a sour grapefruit. Oddly, there is a mild toffee, almost caramel flavor within each sip. Still, it's more like someone decided to further compound the taste by stuffing a Werther's Original (the chewy kind) inside a slice of the sourest grapefruit they could find. Then, after all of this, you realize how much this beer mimics The Asshole Personality. It boasts a whopping 9.4% alcohol per volume guaranteed to turn any well-intentioned person into an asshole should said person decide to have another round. I, for one, never want to put anything even remotely resembling this to my lips and therefore say, "Hell no!"

So from one novice to another, the preceding is a simple way of categorizing your beer. You don't have to be an acolyte, a beer connoisseur, or even a master-beer craftsman to discuss with fluency why you prefer one beer over another. Take a sip, take mental notes of its effect on your senses, and categorize the experience accordingly. But I'd recommend trying this experiment at home first with a beer sampler pack and a notebook. You do, after all, want to avoid the distraction of a pesky holiday party filled with assholes who would be delighted to lord over you their claims that they know the exact taste of a well-balanced beverage of malt and hops. Because you know everyone can go to the produce section of their grocery store and buy hops (whatever that is) so that they can sprinkle it on their salad, toss it into their smoothie, or eat it raw. But malt, in all seriousness, can easily be picked up. Go down the Ethnic aisle of your grocery store and pick up a few bottles labeled "malt beverage," and you will know the precise taste of malt. But, as for everything else, stick to food associations that are familiar to you. Even if some eccentric should look at you like you have a head filled with barley, the nice guy or gal and the life of the party will smile with appreciation that you even dared to describe the taste of beer in simple, everyday language.

Beneath a Cloudy Vacancy

A Poem

Smoke puffs and ponders before
billowing and wisping through a
window
exchanging a cool breeze for the final
grey thoughts of a weary traveler
chewing on the nub of a glowing cigar
that is soon grasped between
the index and middle finger of his
hand
gripping a greying steering wheel
while the other reaches for a mug.

Steam rises with pondering
participation
from the mug filled to the brim
and much too hot to gulp
and weary traveler gags,
thoughtlessly throttled awake
as grey ash plunks down
upon his pant leg
causing him to place down
with speed and care the mug
so as to avoid marking up
the other leg with the piping
stains of a meaningless musing.

Brushing away streaks of grey
carelessness
and dissatisfied with the results
weary traveler takes another go
at his mug and sips,
squinting into the sunny overcast
and seeing, perhaps a mile or so,
the dark seduction of a stormy sky
and he sighs into the air spicy
with rain, exhaust, and cigar smoke.

Drops plunk poignantly upon
the windshield of weary traveler's car
as he takes a deliberating drag
on the soggy remains of a cigar

now unpleasant to puff
and tosses it out the window
and into the air heavy with mist
as the pitter-patter picks up pace
and wind pushes weary traveler's
car from side to side
plunking with rapid speed
drops of rainfall
bringing traffic
to a halting
stop.

The Taxi-Driver

Fiction: Suspense

Drops of rain fell upon a faded grey sedan, labeled Charlie's Cab Company, which sat in an otherwise empty parking lot. Standing next to the car and holding an envelope, Charlie gazed at the grey skies until the rain flowed in tiny creeks between the wrinkles around his eyes and trickled down his cheeks. Driving today would be dreadful.

Last night's final fare occurred because of a choice Charlie made. This choice proved to be dangerous, but not because of his passengers, a young couple recently married.

When the young husband gave out directions, Charlie cringed. He knew the route through the mountains would be treacherous. For a moment, a passing thought urged him to leave the young couple at the restaurant on Main Street. In his brief moment of hesitation, he recalled tales told in his childhood of married couples on dark winding roads. Charlie shook the thought away and smiled at the husband and wife, both of whom teetered on the curb, drunk. Charlie invited them into the cab. The husband helped his giggling wife into her seat before he stumbled his way around the car and got in the back. The wife snuggled next to her husband, closed her eyes, and sighed.

The couple was clearly in love, and Charlie, though distant was his memory of young love, could still relate.

He drove through the fog as Phil, the

name he overheard the wife call her husband, gave directions over the drunken giggles and slurred speech of his wife. Her name, he would later discover, was Alice. As Charlie drove, Phil and Alice sat in the back seat and spoke in whispers occasionally broken by a joke or some story only understood by those riding the buzz of a late-night party. Charlie was glad that Phil was sober enough to guide him around one dark, foggy bend in the back road, then another.

Though short in miles, the trip seemed like an eternity, primarily since Charlie fought to keep sleep from weighing his eyes down. Eventually, he lost the battle as his head bobbed, and his eyes closed. He swerved to the left somewhere between awake and dreaming, then to the right until a horn from an oncoming truck blared.

"You okay, pal?" Phil asked.

Charlie nodded, pinched the bridge of his nose, and continued to drive.

The winding back roads eventually led to a brightly lit mansion upon a hill. As Phil and his wife got out and paid their fare, he placed his hands on the door of the car, leaned into the open window, and whispered.

"Say... buddy... it's late," Phil paused and looked over his shoulder. His wife stumbled over one of the steps leading up to the steps.

"I'm okay," Alice said with a giggle. "Just need to rest for a moment."

Phil looked back at Charlie, then began again. "We thought you might want to come in and sleep in our guest bedroom."

Charlie looked at his watch. 4:05 am. In all his years as a cab driver, no one had ever invited him in. Odd as it was, he was tired and agreed to stay the night.

"Great," Phil smiled. "Can you help me with my wife? Alice had a little too much to drink."

After locking the door and grabbing from the trunk a small duffle bag, which he kept packed for emergencies, Charlie hoisted Alice from one side while her husband did the same on the other. Together, the two men helped a nearly unconscious young bride into the house. After three flights of steps, they laid her in bed and turned off the lights. The two men then headed down four flights of steps, which led down to a basement until they stood in a sparsely, though comfortably furnished little bedroom.

After Phil left the room, Charlie locked the door, shut off the lights, and collapsed on the bed. Sleep overtook his tired body until a bang, and the splintering of wood caused him to stir. As though a part of a bad dream, a blinding light illuminated the hallway and seared through Charlie's closed eyelids. He groaned and attempted to roll over but found himself unable to do so. Upon opening his eyes, Charlie squinted. A flashlight was in his face. Charlie could barely make out the movement of a person just beyond the light.

"Charlie," a distorted voice spoke. "You've been selected."

"Phil? Alice?" Charlie questioned. Charlie couldn't tell whether the voice came from a man or a woman.

"Neither."

"Then where am—"

"Oh, you're still where you've always been," the voice continued. "Only, you've forced us to change the game."

Charlie cleared his throat. He thought back to his most recent fare. Was it only a few hours ago? The only thing he had done differently was accepting the hospitality of two strangers for the night.

"Oh, no," the voice seemed to chuckle. "It wasn't anything you did last night or even the night before. You've just forced our hands."

From somewhere in the darkness, another set of footsteps approached. He heard the ripping of duct tape. Charlie squirmed, but as he did, he found himself held fast by several hands. One set held his wrists, while another set removed blankets, then his t-shirt. A cold metal object placed on his chest caused Charlie to pull away suddenly. The hands held him fast. With deliberate care, another set of hands secured the metal object to his chest with one layer after another layer of tape. As this occurred, the thought running through Charlie's mind was singular. I *hope that I'm around to feel the pain of removing that tape later.*

After his captors shoved his head and arms back into his t-shirt, they hoisted Charlie to his feet and pushed him up the stairs and through a door.

Though blindfolded, Charlie sensed

he was now outside. His captors allowed a brief pause as Charlie pointed his blindfolded eyes toward the sky. Sunlight penetrated through the fabric, yet he was unable to sense the time of day.

How much time passed between last night and this moment? Charlie thought as a heavy hand prodded him forward.

His feet shuffled upon the concrete, then blacktop as his captors led him down a set of steps. Somehow he knew he was still at the mansion.

Breathing a little easier because he had gained his bearings, Charlie was not at all surprised to hear the latch of the driver's side door of his taxicab click open. He was shoved toward the open door and told to sit. He reached for his blindfold.

"Not yet," the distorted voice from before whispered in his ear. "Open your hand."

Charlie complied. A moment later, he held a small square object.

"Not until you hear this phone ring," the voice said. "When it rings, answer it."

The door slammed. Moments passed in silence as Charlie listened. Sensing he was alone, he reached for the blindfold.

The phone rang, and Charlie tore the blindfold from his eyes and tossed it into the backseat. As the phone rang again, he lifted his t-shirt. A black object secured tightly to his chest by duct tape flashed a series of numbers on a small LCD console. Time ticked. The phone rang again. Charlie was sure it had rung several times, so he answered it and hoped he had not pissed off the person on the other end.

An undistorted woman's voice on the other end of the phone spoke first.

"Say a word to the police, and you die. Do you understand?"

"But—"

"Why?" She interrupted. "Simple. You asked for it."

"I don't—"

"Do you understand our demands so far?"

"Yes."

"Good."

Silence.

He lifted his shirt once again. A small red light next to the LCD screen of the box attached to his chest blinked twice.

"No need to check," the woman's voice continued. "We're monitoring your every move. You have 45 minutes to meet our demands. Reach beneath your seat and open the envelope."

Charlie did as he was told and found a white printout paper within the envelope. He unfolded it and read.

Keep the phone on you at all times. You are to go to First National Bank on Main Street and hand the teller, Anna, this yellow envelope. You now have 44 minutes. Destroy this note and be on your way.

Charlie glanced at the box beneath his shirt. Sure enough, 44 minutes remained. He glanced in his rearview mirror, then up toward the mansion. It seemed eerily abandoned. The driveway was empty, and the porch lights were off. No one was in sight.

Perhaps, Charlie thought, *the car Phil and Alice took to the party still sat in a parking garage on Main Street.*

"Charlie," the woman's voice on the phone screamed. "Get moving."

He set the phone down, then buckled his seatbelt and turned the key. The taxi's engine hesitated and conked out. He swore, then turned the key again. He pushed on the gas pedal, and the engine roared. The car squealed as

Charlie sped out of the driveway.

Back on the winding road, which he had been down the night before, Charlie realized the note, now crumpled and damp with sweat, was still clenched in his hand.

Destroy the letter.

He crumpled it into a ball, stuffed it in his mouth, and slowly chewed the paper as he rounded another bend in the road.

Arriving in town, Charlie turned down Main Street, a two-lane one-way road that led north toward several farms owned mostly by Amish families. The next turn he made brought him into the parking lot of First National Bank. Circling the small parking lot so that his car would face the exit, he parked the car and cranked the brake.

A quick lift of his shirt showed ten minutes remained on the LCD screen. His watch showed 9:55 am. He had 5 minutes before the bank would open. He looked up, and large drops of rain began to land on his windshield.

"Great," he muttered. He got out of the car, grabbed the envelope, shoved it beneath his shirt, then closed the door.

For a few moments, Charlie stood in

the rain until it began to trickle down his cheeks. He checked his watch, then looked up at the bank.

"Pleasure. Adventure. Is there a difference?" He smiled, then wiped the tiny creeks of rain from around his eyes. He headed toward the bank as a blonde-haired woman unlocked the front door and held it open for him as he entered.

"Welcome to First National," she said with a smile. "What can we do for you?"

Charlie glanced at her name tag, which read Anna. He handed her the envelope.

As Anna opened the envelope, her smile faded. She locked the door, then signaled to another woman who sat behind a desk in a windowed office. She stood. Charlie turned in her direction and raised his shirt revealing the counter.

00:15:29

The woman inconspicuously hit a button beneath her desk, then stood and smiled.

Sirens blaring in the distance grew

louder as police cars approached the bank. Uniformed officers and a swat team then surrounded the bank.

The telephone held in Charlie's hand rang. He answered it.

"Well done, Charlie," the woman's voice spoke.

"What do you…" Charlie began until he heard a click. "Hello!" He yelled.

The deathly silence of the other end gave him the dreaded answer. He was alone with no recourse upon which to fall. No proof of his coercion.

Later, the local newspaper published Charlie's story on the fifth page of the first section of the Sunday paper with the following headline and corresponding story:

Cab Driver Holds Up Bank with False Bomb. Claims He 'was forced.'

A 57-year-old man was arrested on Tuesday morning as he attempted to rob a bank with a fake bomb strapped to his chest. The retired steelworker turned independent taxi driver maintained that he was abducted early Tuesday morning from the home of his last fare. Upon further investigation, police detectives did determine that he stayed in the basement of a condemned mansion located in the mountains just south of town. Detectives did find DNA and forensic evidence, which indicated that the 57-year-old man lived in the basement of the home for several years. At this time, they have made no connections between the man's most recent activities and the thirty-year-old mansion fire. The mansion, once owned by Phil and Alice Johnson, was condemned. No one knows what happened to the Johnsons.

They Just Don't Stick Around

Fiction: Crime & Suspense

As he knelt in the back storage, Jerry rummaged through a cardboard box, the last one he could find labeled ketchup. He wore his usual red company cap and matching blue shirt with red pinstripes. His job as a shift leader at The Daily Burger was simple: train the new hires, pick up the slack where needed, and keep the kitchen and dining area cleaned and stocked between breakfast, lunch, and dinner. Easy to do, except the only ketchup box he could find was nearly empty. He'd be sure to ask Rhonda, the evening shift supervisor, about this when she came in.

Like most employees at this shitty establishment, necessary items seemed to disappear faster than he could replace them. So did the degreasers Jerry used to clean the cooker hoods every six months. When he went in last month, he discovered the degreasers missing. This discovery amounted to another complaint Jerry documented in his pocket notebook, then later filed with the previous and current management. When that didn't settle the issue, he moved on to upper management, offering simple suggestions, like giving customers what they requested, instead of leaving the condiments out so customers can pick them off like bread tossed out to seagulls. Or keeping commercial-grade solvents under lock and key accessible only to approved staff members. He wrote it up just like that, and he'd say it the same way when the district manager came today on his monthly visit.

Jerry smirked, rehearsing what he planned to say. He'd been at The Daily

Burger for ten years, worked every position available, and even trained some new staff. Still, when Jerry put in for a promotion a few months ago, upper management overlooked him. He didn't understand their rationale, but he certainly had something to say about it. With that thought buzzing in his mind, Jerry stood and stretched, then pulled out his pocket notebook and flipped it open to the next blank page. Nearly full, the notebook contained a month's worth of issues he had observed and documented. Some issues dealt explicitly with the new manager the company brought on to "clean things up."

As he jotted down notes about the missing ketchup, he kept an ear out for the kitchen staff. Not that he was worried they'd need his help. The breakfast crew was cleaning up, and the only remaining patrons were the low-maintenance elderly regulars. Every day they stayed until noon, sipping their coffee and reminiscing about "the good old days." Jerry shook his head and smirked, hoping he wouldn't live long enough to remember his current "good old days."

Stuffing the notepad away and kneeling, Jerry lifted the cardboard box. Turning, he bumped into the new store manager, an overweight man with balding dark hair and a thick greying mustache.

"Sorry, Bennie," Jerry said.

Mustache twitching, Bennie glared at Jerry through thick glasses and grunted. "You about done with that?"

"Yes," Jerry said, sure to look his boss in those beady eyes.

Bennie crossed his arms. "I've been watching you, son. It might be my first month here, but I've seen things at this store I don't like."

Jerry swallowed down a snarky remark and smiled. "I'm glad someone's noticed. Did you know the ketchup is nearly gone, and it's only Tuesday?"

Bennie narrowed his eyes. "Did you check the loading dock? The freezer?"

Jerry shrugged. "I logged those supplies in myself last week. When I came in this morning, this is all that was left." Jerry shoved the box toward Bennie.

Bennie reached into the box and took a handful of ketchup packets. These he carefully inspected before releasing them.

"Right," Bennie said. He lowered his voice. "Don't say anything about this when Antonio comes in. You understand?"

Something heavy and metallic clanged. Both men glanced toward the kitchen. With raised eyebrows, Bennie turned back toward Jerry.

"I understand," Jerry said. "Now, if you don't mind. I've got some restocking to do."

Bennie stepped aside. As Jerry passed, he avoided further eye contact with his boss. Being brought into Bennie's confidence after a month seemed odd to Jerry. Perhaps it had something to do with their district manager, Antonio Cruz, coming sometime today. Whatever the case, Jerry had no intention of holding back on the issues he'd noted about Bennie. This man, as demonstrated, seemed to hover over the workers, doing more to inhibit, rather than promote, productivity.

On top of that, Bennie should've ordered twice as much ketchup as the store generally needed. Jerry knew he could do a better job than this hack. Somehow, he needed to convince Antonio to give him a chance to prove himself.

Once he passed into the dining area, Jerry turned and winked at the newly hired girl with long braids working the register. With a smile, she averted her eyes and returned to wiping the counter and restocking the napkin dispenser. Passing her on the way to the self-serve counter, Jerry caught her eyes and smiled slyly.

"What's up with you?" she asked.

"You'll see." Jerry sauntered past and dropped the box next to the condiment dispensers.

As he began to shovel out handfuls of ketchup packets, Jerry mentally kicked himself. Though he had trained the girl, he couldn't remember her name. To Jerry's credit, however, the turn-over rate at this story was so high, he hadn't bothered to get to know any of the new hires. But there was something special about this girl. His lips moved, recalling her name began with a *sh*.

Perhaps Cheryl or Shonda. No, it was something fancier than that. He wanted to compliment the new girl, to tell her he liked the way—

Fuck it.

Jerry turned. "Excuse—"

Bennie stood behind him, arms crossed as if condemning Jerry for his lack of effort to learn the names of coworkers.

Over Bennie's shoulder, the new girl covered her mouth, stifling a laugh while catching Bennie's attention.

"Shakira," Bennie said. "I'm glad we're entertaining you. Now, isn't there a counter you need to clean?"

Choking back laughter, Shakira grabbed a spray bottle and a rag while Jerry managed to compose himself. Shakira flashed Jerry a grin.

Turning his attention back to Jerry, Bennie huffed. "If you're done here, take care of the trash." He made a sweeping gesture toward the dining area. "And do try to get the floor mopped. This place is a mess." A few patrons looked up, and Bennie casually strolled over to them.

As Bennie hobnobbed with the customers, Jerry gritted his teeth and began to collect the trash. He always greeted the customers at this time of day while someone else typically took care of the trash. But that employee hadn't shown up.

Management needed to hold lazy employees accountable. Instead, they expected Jerry to pick up the slack. Jerry had had just about enough. He wanted to say as much to Bennie's face, but that would mean looking for another job while simultaneously making a fool of himself in front of the regular customers. Besides, he'd already complained about micromanagement. Surely Antonio got wind of that.

Jerry dropped the fourth bag of trash into a pile by the door. One of the customers, an older woman, accompanied by a man about her age, spoke up. "You're doing a fine job."

"Thanks," Jerry said. "It's nice to know someone has noticed."

"Oh. I'm sure your boss has," the elderly woman said. "You keep this place clean enough."

Jerry nodded, the phrase *clean enough,* sticking in his mind. "Well, I hope you enjoy the meal more than you enjoy the cleanliness of The Daily Burger."

After gathering up the last of the trash, Jerry headed toward the side door. Maybe he wasn't doing the best job, but it was a little hard to do that when every shift was shorted by at least one employee most of the time. Maybe Bennie, or the company, was just cheap.

"Did you hear that, Jerry?" Shakira called out.

Jerry froze. "What's that?"

Shakira placed her hands on the counter and leaned forward. "The place. You keep it clean enough."

Jerry lingered on Shakira's curves for a moment. "Right. Clean enough. I'll be back in a bit. Shakira."

"Cool!" Shakira said. "I'll be here."

Feeling the warmth of embarrassment, Jerry pushed open the glass door. He didn't know what to make of Shakira, and he had a mind to figure her out, though he was pretty sure The Daily Burger would have something to say about shift leaders fraternizing with part-time employees.

In the parking lot, a fit, middle-aged man dressed in a power suit and tie stepped out of a dark blue BMW. He carried a briefcase, and he seemed to scrutinize the parking lot as he approached the restaurant.

Setting the trash down, Jerry waved. "Antonio. Welcome!"

Antonio paused. "Jeffrey. How are you?"

Jerry reached out his hand. "Jerry. I'm doing fine."

Nodding, Antonio ignored Jerry's offered hand and reached for the door. Jerry beat him to the handle and, stepping aside, opened the door.

When Antonio passed into the vestibule, Jerry said, "Have a nice day, sir."

Receiving no acknowledgment from the district manager, Jerry released the door and gathered up the trash once again.

"What an ass," Jerry grumbled. Then he wondered what choice words the district manager would have for him. Jerry first met Antonio close to five years ago and had thirty or more interactions with the man. By this time, Antonio should at least know the name of one of the most tenured employees at this particular location of The Daily Burger, especially since that same employee kept tabs on almost all that went on at the restaurant.

Jerry hoisted trash into the dumpsters, imagining each bag representing his aspirations for leveling up in his career. There wasn't much going for him in this rink-a-dink, middle-of-nowhere town, not with factory jobs going away. He laid nearly his entire future on the notion of one day bringing home forty-five thousand a year, plus retirement. That would also make him a little more desirable to the ladies looking for a little more than a good lay now and then.

Thinking of Shakira, Jerry grinned and tossed the last of the trash into the dumpster. As he did, the bag ripped. Jumping away, Jerry cursed as a concoction of grease, soda, and coffee sprayed his pant legs.

With a glance, Jerry confirmed no one else had been in the parking lot to witness his blunder. He scooped up the larger pieces of trash, tossed them away, then kicked the rest underneath the dumpster. With that settled, he wiped his hands onto his uniform and grabbed a pack of cigarettes.

After lighting up, he took a slow drag. God! He needed that. With Antonio here, and the lunch crowd arriving soon, his next break wouldn't be for another three hours.

Tires squealed. A moment later, a

faded blue Oldsmobile pulled into the parking lot. Jerry cringed. Rhonda, the busty redheaded evening shift supervisor, was almost always late. The Oldsmobile came to a stop right next to Jerry as the window rolled down.

"Hey, Jer," Rhonda said. She gave Jerry a once over. "What happened to you?"

He shrugged and took another drag on his cigarette. "Antonio's here."

"Shit!" Rhonda said. "Ya could've warned me."

"Consider yourself warned," Jerry said. "The memo's been posted for almost a week."

Rhonda eyed the cigarette. "Save me a hit. I'm gonna need it."

She cranked the car into reverse and backed into the parking space right next to the BMW. The driver's side door opened, and Rhonda climbed out. Though ten years older than Jerry, Rhonda's clear skin suggested a healthy diet, none of which consisted of the shit food served in this establishment. After slamming the door behind her, Rhonda approached Jerry, her breasts swaying loosely beneath the black camisole she wore. She had The Daily Burger's work shirt crumpled and slung lazily over her shoulder.

Once toe-to-toe with Jerry, Rhonda grinned. "Doesn't take a psychologist to know what you're thinking." She plucked the cigarette from Jerry's mouth and took a drag.

Rhonda played a variation of this game with him damn near every day.

Jerry cleared his throat. "It also won't take Antonio more than two seconds to fire your ass if he sees you like this."

"You'd like that," Rhonda said. Pressing against him, she blew smoke in his face. She handed him the last of the cigarette. "Here. Finish this off, will ya?"

Jerry parted his lips, and Rhonda held the butt there until he took another drag. Jerry held the smoke in, riding out a slight nicotine buzz. He exhaled through the side of his mouth.

"Another thing," Jerry said. "The ketchup is nearly out. What happened to the other boxes?"

Rhonda wrapped her arm around his back. "Which box do you want to talk about?"

Jerry pushed her away.

Rhonda frowned. "You're no fun."

"You try to placate Bennie and Antonio at the same time," Jerry said.

Rhonda rolled her eyes. "'kay. Better see what this is all about." She turned, pulling her shirt on and buttoning it as she approached the entrance.

"See you on the other side," Jerry said.

Rhonda flipped him the bird and disappeared into the restaurant. Jerry chuckled. In any other environment, they'd have filed charges of sexual harassment against each other. With Rhonda as his supervisor, he'd probably win. Still, he was almost certain this was just a game to her, something that meant absolutely nothing. He never took her advances too seriously. But that didn't keep him from indulging just enough to satisfy his little flights of fancy.

Before heading inside, Jerry took a seat on the curb and enjoyed another cigarette. As he did, he took out his pocket notebook. Skimming through the pages, Jerry paused to dog-ear some incidents and infractions. Though Antonio may not know his name, he knew the complaints. Jerry would be prepared when the distract manager asked for more detail. Jerry grinned. That would also be a great time to ask about the application he put in for assistant store manager. Jerry had already outperformed Rhonda. A few months ago, he even temporarily performed the job of a store manager when the last one left without warning. Jerry glanced at the block lettering beneath the restaurant's roadway sign. The *t* was missing, so the sign read *Now Hiring Sore Managers*. That about summed it up for this place. But he wouldn't be a "sore" manager if they gave him the job. They wouldn't put just anyone in as a trainer or a shift lead. He knew every job and did them damn well. And those under his charge performed their duties better than most. He was a shoo-in for the store management position, and he'd be sure to tell Antonio that, too.

When he returned to his shift, Jerry wasn't surprised to see a line, nor was he surprised to see Shakira handling that line with ease. He'd trained her, after all. But Jerry was surprised that Rhonda, Bennie, and Antonio were not in the dining area. If he were a district manager, that's where he would focus his efforts to get this place running like "the well-oiled machine" those training videos promised.

On his way into the kitchen, Jerry paused behind the counter. Shakira punched in an order, rang a customer up, then turned to Jerry.

"They're in the office," Shakira said, then crinkled her nose as she took a step back. "Boy, you look a mess. You better get cleaned up before working the rest of your shift."

Jerry looked down and realized how unpresentable his uniform had become after the garbage incident.

A smartly dressed woman spoke up. "If you don't mind, I'd like to order."

Jerry grinned. "Right. Sorry about that. Excuse me a second." He reached over and punched a code into the register. "Manager's discount. Enjoy your meal."

Passing through the kitchen, Jerry noted they'd be short-staffed. But he'd bounce between the front and the kitchen, working both at the same time, if needed.

"Give me a sec," he called in the kitchen, then dashed toward his locker. He grabbed the spare uniform he kept on hand in case of emergencies. Yet another thing he hoped to make known to Antonio.

After a quick change and a splash of his face in the bathroom, Jerry carried a neatly folded, though terribly soiled uniform back to his locker. As he did so, he passed the store manager's office. In his earlier haste, Jerry hadn't given the office much thought, especially because of his previously poor appearance. This time, he paused. Leaning in, he cupped his hands against the steel door.

Voices, muffled and incoherent, came from the other side of the office. Rhonda was yelling. He strained to make out her words, but that was cut short by the distinct click of the door release. Jerry stepped back as the door swung open.

Bennie glared at him. "Can I help you?"

"Uh. Sorry to interrupt. But we're gonna need all hands on deck in a bit," Jerry said. He caught a glimpse of Rhonda, a scowl on her face. She didn't look up.

"Is that all?" Bennie asked. His mustache twitched, almost daring Jerry to add more detail.

Jerry took a step back and waved.

"Just wanted to let you know, but we've got it covered until—"

The door slammed shut. Whatever was going on, Jerry expected Rhonda to give him an earful sometime after Bennie and Antonio left.

Shouting from the dining area drew Jerry's attention. He fumbled with his soiled uniform, then tossed it toward the lockers. That could wait. At the moment, he needed to attend to something far more pressing.

When he returned to the dining area, Jerry saw the problem. A woman with two small children demanded to speak to the manager. Though Shakira seemed to remain calm, her tight-lipped smile told a different story.

Jerry stepped in. "Excuse me, Ma'am. What seems to be the problem?"

The woman glanced at Jerry's name tag and scowled. "Jerry, is it? Are you the store manager?"

"I am the shift leader," Jerry said.

"Shift leader, huh?" The woman directed her attention to the other patrons in line. "See this? I've got the shift leader. Fine!"

Jerry concluded this woman probably had poor customer service everywhere she went, but he left that one alone.

The woman turned back to Jerry. "Well, *Jerry, the shift leader*." She gestured toward Shakira. "This girl you've hired rang up our order three times. Each time, it was way overpriced."

Shakira retorted, "It wasn't—"

"Let me see," Jerry said, cutting Shakira off as he took a look at the register. "It says here you ordered two kid's meals with the toys, plus a Deluxe Daily Burger, correct?"

"That's right," the woman said. "It shouldn't be—"

"Thirty-one fifty-seven," Jerry said. "I've worked here for ten years. That's the price."

The woman scrunched up her face. "That can't be right."

In his peripheral, Jerry spotted a customer in the back of the line leaving the store. "Ma'am, perhaps we can step aside and—"

"Lose my place?" The woman asked. "Is that what you were going to say?" By her side, the woman's children started to cry. Another customer left the store.

Just then, Bennie stepped in. "Jerry,

I'll handle it from here. Shakira, why don't you take five minutes?"

Jerry pushed through the kitchen doors, and Shakira followed right behind him. As the doors swung shut, the woman began to say something about how good help was so hard to find.

Shakira grabbed Jerry by the arm. "I don't know what I did wrong."

Jerry turned to see tears filling Shakira's eyes.

"Listen," Jerry said. "You've been here a week, and you're doing a damn good job. She isn't the first customer to complain about the prices, nor will she be the last."

Shakira sniffed. "Really?"

From the kitchen, someone shouted. "Running out of nuggets!"

Jerry looked at Shakira. "Really, I mean it. You're the best I've trained. I hope you stick around. How are you feeling?"

"I'm good," Shakira said.

"Need more fries," someone else in the kitchen called.

"Alright," Jerry said. "I've got to take care of that. Talk to you later, okay?"

While Shakira returned to the cash

registers, Jerry headed into the kitchen. On his way, an acne-faced teen darted past him.

"Sorry," the teen called out.

"Don't forget the nuggets!" Someone else called.

Jerry took a peek in the kitchen. One of his recent trainees seemed to maneuver with ease between the fryers and the grill.

"Be in a second," Jerry said, then followed the frantic teen to the freezer.

As he reached for the handle, the door swung open, and a box of fries hit Jerry in the gut. He gasped out a curse as the teen's face grew another shade of red.

"I'm sorry, I didn't..." The teen's voice trailed off as he adjusted his grip on the box.

"Don't. Worry. About it," Jerry said between breaths. "Did you. Get. The nuggets?"

"We're all out," the teen said.

Jerry clutched his gut as he took another moment. "Okay. Let me check."

The teen headed off, leaving Jerry to investigate the freezer on his own. As he reached for the door, someone behind him cleared his throat. Jerry turned.

Bennie's mustache twitched. "All good in the front. How's everything in the back?"

"The kid says the nuggets are missing," Jerry said. "I was just going to—"

Bennie stormed past Jerry and yanked the freezer door open. Jerry followed him inside.

The shelves were layered two deep and two high with an assortment of boxes and bags of burgers and fries.

Bennie grunted, "Did the kid check behind the burgers?"

Jerry went in for a closer look. He lifted and placed a few items on the floor. Though he oversaw the restock of inventory, it was possible someone from the evening shift rearranged things.

"There," Bennie said when Jerry stood up.

Jerry glanced at the shelf empty save for a scattering of frozen nuggets. Jerry picked one up and showed it to his boss.

"Don't worry," Jerry said. "I'll get to the bottom of this today."

Bennie swiped at his mustache and sniffed. "I have no doubt you will, which makes for an interesting segue into our meeting with Antonio. When you finish up here, meet us in the office, okay?" Bennie turned on his heels and exited the freezer.

Jerry rummaged through the burgers and fries, arranging and rearranging the boxes. When he finished, he placed his hands on his hips and glanced around. Having checked in all the inventory on Thursday, he couldn't understand what had happened. Especially since there was a surplus just two days ago. There must've been—

He paused, spotting what looked like a dark, irregular-shaped blotch in the corner of the freezer floor. Jerry placed the bags he held back on the shelf. As he knelt, he inspected the irregularity more closely. Jerry determined it was a puddle of some kind, and upon touching discovered it was thick and sticky. He placed his finger under his nose and smelled the coppery scent of blood. This puddle wasn't there yesterday afternoon, which meant someone was super careless last night.

Standing upright, Jerry quickly inspected each box and bag to see if the leakage came from the inventory currently stocked in the freezing. Finding nothing as he replaced the last of the items, Jerry speculated on what could have happened after he left last night. Perhaps the freezer had thawed slightly, or perhaps someone cut open a defrosted bag of patties. Whatever the case, he'd ask Rhonda the next time he saw her. Before doing so, he'd make the clean-up job a little easier by sprinkling some all-purpose cleaning solution over the congealed puddle.

On his way to the custodial closet, Jerry shot a glance at the kitchen staff. The acne-faced teen handled things nicely at the final packing station, and the other employee still moved gracefully between the grill and the fryers. Jerry grinned, knowing he'd done his job of training both of them well. They'd be fine for a few minutes.

Behind him, someone grabbed Jerry's arm, dragging him toward the utility closet.

"Jer," Rhonda hissed. "I need to talk to you, like, now."

Rhonda yanked Jerry into the closet and slammed the door shut.

In the darkness, Rhonda pressed against Jerry. The sweet scent of fresh perfume filled Jerry's nostrils, and blood rushed to his groin.

"Oh," Rhonda cooed. "You like that."

"Involuntary," Jerry offered.

"Tease," Rhonda said as she stepped back. "Did Bennie talk to you?"

Jerry rubbed the back of his neck. "Yeah. What happened last night?"

Rhonda searched Jerry's eyes. "I closed up as usual. Why?"

"Nuggets are missing and something bloody spilled in the freezer," Jerry said.

Rhonda mouthed Jerry's words back to him as her eyes seemed to glaze over. Her lips stopped, and she cocked a glance at Jerry.

"Shit!" Rhonda said. "I thought I — Did Bennie see?"

"I don't think so," Jerry said. He grabbed her, pulling her close. "Listen, Rhonda. I don't know what's going on, but your carelessness is going to get me in trouble."

Rhonda pushed him away. "You? What about me? Tell me about that work of fiction you're working on." She pointed at Jerry's breast pocket.

He shielded his pocket as if protecting the precious safeguard he'd created for himself.

Rhonda gave him a one-handed shove. "You and your notes."

"Maybe you should try it," Jerry said.

Rhonda narrowed her eyes. "Who says I haven't?"

Jerry looked away. "Just get it cleaned up. Okay?"

Rhonda leaned in. Brushing her lips against Jerry's ear, she whispered, "Oh. I thought you'd like it dirty."

Jerry flushed as he choked on a few words.

Rhonda took a step back and laughed. "I gotcha, Jer. I'll take care of it. Now go!"

The utility closet popped open, and Rhonda shoved Jerry back into the hallway. Disoriented, Jerry headed toward the office while Rhonda sashayed to the front counter.

Jerry sat in the office, willing down a stiffy. Whatever Rhonda was playing at, Jerry planned to demand an explanation later. Across from Jerry, Bennie and Antonio scrutinized him from behind the desk. Bennie stood just behind Antonio, who sat at the desk.

For now, Jerry decided he'd hold back on letting them know about the mess in the freezer. He pulled out his pocket notebook, ready to lead in with the issues he logged about the ketchup and the degreaser.

Antonio raised a hand. "You won't be needing that, Jeffrey."

"It's Jerry, sir," Jerry said.

Antonio glanced at Bennie, who nodded.

"Sorry," Antonio said. He shuffled through some papers. "It seems you've lodged several complaints about this establishment and applied to be an assistant store manager." Antonio paused, glanced at a paper, then looked Jerry in the eyes. "You've applied for promotion four times. Is that right?"

"That's right, sir," Jerry said. "I've been at this for ten years, and— "

"Nine years and two months," Bennie interrupted.

Asshole, Jerry thought as he forced a smile. "Still, I've trained the entire staff and filled in as a store manager. That is until Bennie came on. I think— "

"I know about all that," Antonio interrupted. "Your record is impeccable. This is why we are bringing you in on this little project."

"Pardon me?" Jerry asked.

Bennie stepped forward. For a moment, he rubbed his mustache. "When I said I've been watching you, I meant it. You're a fine employee. I'm damn proud to have you on staff at one of my restaurants."

Jerry's head seemed to spin. "Wait! Is this some kind of undercover boss thing?" He glanced at the four corners of the office. "Where's the hidden camera? I didn't sign up for this."

"Relax," Bennie said. "You're not being recorded. You may know me as Benjamin Jones." Bennie pinched the tip of his mustache and yanked it off. "God, that was getting annoying."

Jerry stared at Bennie, who massaged his bare upper lip.

"Wait," Jerry said. "Aren't you—"

"The owner of The Daily Burger," Bennie said. "That's right. You've got a very keen eye, and we've noted all of your complaints. This is the worst of the chains."

Jerry wondered how terrible the other chains were if this one was the worst. He didn't ask this as he waited for Bennie, or Antonio, to continue.

Bennie gestured toward Antonio. "Antonio and I went into this venture fifteen years ago. All of our stores are doing great, except for this one. We're thinking about shutting it down."

As if rehearsed, Antonio picked up the lead-in. "But we're also pretty sure you're the man to identify two of the issues we are having."

"The loss," Jerry offered. He checked Antonio's and Bennie's reactions. They glanced at each other. A slight twinkle in their eyes suggested he'd hit it right on the head. Jerry continued. "And our issue with staff retention."

"That's right," Bennie said. "People seem to just leave without notice."

"We think it has something to do with Rhonda," Antonio offered.

Jerry thought about that for a moment. Rhonda, by his estimation, was a little rough around the edges. But she was fun to have around, and the customers seemed to respond well to her. "I don't see—"

Antonio held up a hand. "Now that you know. We need you to keep an eye on Rhonda."

"Before you say yes," Bennie picked up. "It'll require some overtime, which we don't mind paying. You can do that for us, right?"

Jerry checked the four corners of the office, just to be sure he wasn't on Candid Camera or something. He wiped a sweaty palm on a pant leg. "What exactly is it you want me to watch for?"

"We're pretty sure you know," Antonio said.

Glancing from Antonio to Bennie, Jerry realized these men had already made up their minds. On top of that, he couldn't help but feel a sense of satisfaction that his hard work had not gone unnoticed. He thought of the missing inventory and the plethora of complaints he had filed in the last few years. Though he couldn't prove it, Rhonda had to be the culprit if the owners of The Daily Burger bothered to come all this way to recruit him. Rhonda and her flirtatious games were coming to an end even without his help.

"What's in it for me?" Jerry asked.

Bennie rubbed at his upper lip as he glanced at Antonio.

Antonio nodded. "How about a promotion and a pay raise. That's something you would like, isn't it?"

"And moving expenses," Jerry added.

Bennie raised an eyebrow. "For what?"

"You're closing this place down, aren't you?" Jerry asked. "I'm going to have to move to a different store, right?"

"Consider it done," Antonio said. "I'll personally see to your relocation."

"Sounds like a plan," Bennie said, stepping forward and extending a hand to Jerry.

Jerry stood, a plan to trap Rhonda already forming in his mind. He gripped Bennie's hand. "I'll get on it tonight."

"We hoped you'd say that," Bennie said.

Antonio stood. "Get it done sooner rather than later, and you'll be promoted for sure."

Jerry exchanged a handshake with Antonio. This little partnership he had with Rhonda these past three years was over, of that Jerry was certain.

As expected, Jerry found himself busy for the next three hours filling in at the fryer, the grill, and even the drive-up window. None of this he minded as it kept him busy while he plotted exactly how he'd position Rhonda to get rid of her. Bennie and Antonio were convinced she was the cause of the consistent shortage, though they had nothing more than raw data and speculation.

Jerry only knew Rhonda had gotten sloppy. He could stomach petty theft. But he couldn't stand a grimy store. He worked too hard to oversee the cleaning of the place. So much so, he often did it himself rather than entrust the job to a newbie. That puddle of blood he discovered was something new.

He knew what he would do when he got off shift. He'd wait in the shadows, then confront Rhonda. First, he'd ask her to open the massive trunk of that Oldsmobile. He grinned at that thought, wondering if she'd pick up on the innuendo. After finding the stolen items in the trunk, he knew he'd have her. That's when he'd get her to come clean about the congealed blood he'd found in the freezer.

Long after Jerry's shift should've ended, he beelined it to the lockers, picked up his soiled uniform, and grabbed his street clothes. He didn't intend to stay until closing, but Shakira suddenly had to leave early. So did the acne-faced teen in the kitchen. It was a long day, and he looked forward to a stiff drink at home. What he had planned for tonight would have to wait until tomorrow. He headed to the bathroom. As he took off his pants, the door flung open.

"Hey, Jer," Rhonda said. A mischievous grin passed over her face. "Oh, I've caught you at the right time."

"Rhonda," Jerry said, pulling his pants up.

"Don't worry about that," Rhonda said. As she approached, she used one hand to unbutton her shirt. "It's just you and me."

Jerry paused. "I didn't see Bennie or Antonio leave."

Rhonda raised an eyebrow and smirked. "Oh. They left right about the time you busied yourself with the fryers."

Jerry's eyes wandered to Rhonda's cleavage. "Where does that leave us?"

Rhonda approached. "That depends, Jerry. What did you boys talk about?"

Jerry stuttered. "Just, um, possible promotion."

Rhonda stripped off her work shirt. "You know, we had a good thing going."

Jerry shrugged as he fastened the button of his pants. "They already have you pegged, Rhonda."

Rhonda froze. "How so?"

"They think you're the one stealing shit from the store," Jerry blurted out.

Rhonda raised an eyebrow, and a smirk played at the corner of her lips. Jerry hadn't anticipated this reaction.

"Why don't I show you what we've been cooking up?" Rhonda asked. She turned, and Jerry stared, mouth agape as Rhonda walked out the door. She stopped. "You coming, or what?"

Jerry followed Rhonda out into the parking lot, stopping at the Oldsmobile.

Rhonda faced him, hands on hips and legs shoulder-width apart. "Go ahead. Pop the trunk."

Jerry eyed her as he reached for the trunk.

"But you should know the reason," Rhonda said. "I think I owe ya that."

Removing his hand from the trunk latch, Jerry gave Rhonda his full attention. "What're you getting at?"

Rhonda stepped forward. "I liked you, Jerry. I really did. But you just wouldn't stop with the complaints."

"What do you—"

Someone grabbed Jerry from behind, plunging something sharp into his neck. Jerry spun.

Antonio greeted Jerry with a grin. "It was all a ruse, Jeffrey."

Disoriented, Jerry grabbed at the car in a vain attempt to keep himself upright.

"Everything," Antonio continued. "I got tired of your complaints. That's when I convinced Bennie to come out and—"

Jerry slumped to the pavement. His eyes glazed over as he panted for breath.

"That's how you take out a man!" Antonio boasted. He directed his attention to Rhonda. "Not whatever you did in the freezer last night."

"Oh. Is it hurting him?" Rhonda asked.

"I don't think so," Antonio said. He kicked Jerry's leg. "Jeffrey, can you feel anything?"

Jerry choked.

"Tony, this is bad," Rhonda said. "You sure we can't bring him in?"

"Rhonda," Antonio said. "It's a little too late for that. Now pop the trunk."

Rhonda did so. "Is this good enough?"

Antonio peered inside the trunk. "Perfect. Where'd you get the plastic?"

"Over the state line," Rhonda said. She glanced down at Jerry. "It's a shame, though. What're ya gonna tell Bennie?"

"Good employees," Antonio shrugged. "They just don't stick around."

Author's Notes

In compiling this eclectic work I so aptly named, *A Crock of Sundries,* I sought to bring you some of my best work and some of my work that desperately needed major editing and revising before making it into this little book. Perhaps this collection serves as a reason to polish up some of my less refined work. Or, more accurately, a reason for waylaying my progress on my lengthier pieces. Nonetheless, I desired to arrange the literature thematically rather than presenting it in the order they were written or by type. I hope I achieved this effect.

Generations, My Not Favorite Teacher, Unbuttoned, One Hundred Words, Beneath a Cloudy Vacancy, A Heretical Guide to Classifying Beer, The Caged Bird, Vitality, and *A Winter's Siege* were all written between 2016 and 2019 as a part of my graduate program in Creative Writing and Literature for Teachers at Fairleigh Dickinson University. *Unbuttoned* and *A Winter's Siege* are both very fictionalized accounts of some of my experiences growing up. *Unbuttoned,* as you read, centers on the complexities of navigating potentially romantic relationships. I had high hopes of writing this as a full-length novel. But I am satisfied in its present state. Similarly, I had aspirations for creating *A Winter's Siege* as a full-length play, but that has yet to pan out.

I initially wrote *I, Lamppost, Ponder, They Just Don't Stick Around, A Froggy Will,* and *The Taxi-Driver* before 2016. Some made it to the blog between 2015 and 2019 when I first started my journey to publication. *The Taxi-Driver* and *Unbuttoned* were published in *Second Sojourn* (2019), a collection of work by some amazing authors local to Harford County and some of the surrounding counties in Maryland. These stories, along with *A Heretical Guide for Classifying Beer,* found their way in another anthology put out by Indies United, *Infinite Indies* (2020). As previously published literary works, they also needed a little more tweaking. Because, in reality, is a piece of writing ever really finished?

The Taxi-Driver and *They Just Don't Stick Around* were both inspired by two bizarre police blotters. They are my attempts to understand exactly how one could get themselves to such a messed-up situation. The writing process for *They Just Don't Stick Around* began in 2016, then halted for lack of interest for about six years. Editing and completing the piece was equal parts pleasure and pain, and a whole part of a love for the guy I was as represented in my writing. Special thanks to Bel Air Creative Writer's Society members Bob Broomall, Keith Hoskins, Alan Amrine, and Kim Monaco for your valuable feedback. I hope you love the final draft.

Now, dear reader, I leave you to further speculate ponder the situations that inspired the writings while revealing there are more parts to *A Froggy Will* than what I've included in this little collection. Where there is a volume one, there will most certainly be a volume two.

If you enjoyed *A Crock of Sundries, Volume 1,* or simply want to drop me your critique, please do so whichever platform you purchased this book. Reviews are incredibly valuable for getting the work of independent authors noticed. Also, I am incredibly active on Goodreads, and I would be thrilled to see your comments posted there.

About the Author

Tim grew up in Syracuse, New York. He currently resides in Maryland where he teaches English, Creative Writing, Film, and Theatre on the middle school level. At the insistence of his own students, he began writing seriously in 2014.

He credits his love for story to his mother, who spent countless hours reading to him and his siblings when they were growing up. Growing up, he devoured the literary words of C. S. Lewis, J. R. R. Tolkien, Piers Anthony, and many others. Mysteries, thrillers, and fantasies are among the genre he most frequently reads.

When he's not writing, he's reading, teaching, camping, or enjoying a live music concert.

Connect with Tim

www.timothyrbaldwin.com

facebook.com/timothyrbaldwin

instagram.com/timothyrbaldwin

twitter.com/timothyrbaldwin

www.goodreads.com/author/show/19140216

Sign up for the newsletter
https://bit.ly/3wtX3vT

Also by Timothy R. Baldwin

A Kahale and Claude Mystery Series

Book 1: Camp Lenape (2019)
Book 2: Shadows of Doubt (2020)
Book 2.5: A Bazaar Christmas (2020)
Book 3: Operation Varsity Blues (2020)

A Shot in the Dark Series

Book 1: A Shot at Mercy (2021)

These and more at
https://www.indiesunited.net/timothy-baldwin

About Indies United Publishing House

Greetings my fellow Indie authors and avid readers to what, I hope with your help, will become a thriving community where authors and readers can meet, support and encourage one another.

Here at Indies United, we are a co-op of like-minded authors working together to showcase our books, and our diversity as writers, that embrace over a dozen different genres. We openly encourage and support both new and established authors in their pursuit of finding their audience while bringing to you books worth reading.

Most traditional publishing venues are like a very nice formal dinner party where everything is planned and always follows the same formula. The food is generally good, the entertainment acceptable without being distracting, the conversation predictable, the event exclusive, and always formal. Indie publishing is more like going to a block party. The food is still good, but everyone brings to the table something from their own kitchen, the music is lively, the attire is generally casual, and you never know who you'll meet or what they may say when you do.

But in this vibrant world of Indie publishing, many authors languish, not because the books they produce are bad, but because the industry itself is stacked against them. Individual voices are easily lost in the din of advertising and most Indies can never hope to compete on the same level as a house author with all their backing. I wanted to change that, and so I created Indies United, to give those authors a home to call their own and bring fresh, innovative, and exciting books to readers all over the world.

Welcome to our block party.

www.indiesunited.net

Timothy R. Baldwin

www.ingramcontent.com/pod-product-compliance
Lightning Source LLC
Chambersburg PA
CBHW050331110726
47899CB00007B/2458

9781644563458